where
love
begins

ALSO BY JUDITH HERMANN

The Summer House, Later
Nothing But Ghosts
Alice

where love begins

JUDITH HERMANN

Translated from the German by
Margot Bettauer Dembo

THE CLERKENWELL PRESS

Published in Great Britain in 2016 by
THE CLERKENWELL PRESS
An imprint of Profile Books Ltd
3 Holford Yard
Bevin Way
London WC1X 9HD
www.profilebooks.com

First published by Fischer Verlag, Germany
Copyright © Judith Hermann, 2014, 2016
Translation copyright © Margot Bettauer Dembo, 2016

The translation of this work was supported by a grant from the Goethe-Institut which is
funded by the German Ministry of Foreign Affairs

10 9 8 7 6 5 4 3 2 1

Printed and bound by CPI Group
(UK) Ltd, Croydon, CR0 4YY

The moral right of the author has been asserted.

Typeset by MacGuru Ltd in Granjon
info@macguru.org.uk

A CIP catalogue record for this book is available from the British Library.

ISBN 978 1 78125 470 7
eISBN 978 1 78283 170 9

MIX
Paper from
responsible sources
FSC
www.fsc.org FSC® C020471

For Amad

It's like this – Stella and Jason meet on an airplane. A propeller plane, not a long flight. Stella was coming from Clara's wedding. She caught the bridal bouquet, that's probably why she's so distraught; and she had to say goodbye to Clara, that's why she's feeling so forlorn. It was a beautiful wedding. From now on Stella is on her own. Jason was coming from a construction site. He was laying tiles, that's why he's so dusty. And he worked all night long, driving to the airport at the crack of dawn; that's why he's so tired. The job is finished; he'll be looking for a new job. Fate, or whoever, has seated Stella next to Jason, row 7, seats A and C. Stella will save the boarding pass for many years. For many years. Jason is sitting by the window; the seat next to him is empty. Stella's seat is on the aisle, but in spite of that she sits down next to Jason. She can't help it.

Jason is tall and lean, unshaven; his black hair is grey because of the dust. He's wearing a rough woollen jacket and dirty jeans. He looks at Stella as if she'd taken leave of her senses, looks at her angrily; she startles him. So direct, so unceremonious. Nothing that could have been dragged out. If Stella hadn't caught Clara's bridal bouquet – jasmine and lilacs, a luxuriant abundance tied with a silken ribbon – she wouldn't be so breathless. Glowing cheeks, a shocking lack of detachment.

Stella, my name is Stella.

She says, I'm afraid of flying. I don't do well flying. May I sit next to you; please, could I just stay here sitting next to you.

It's the truth. Jason's expression changes; it doesn't exactly soften, but it changes. He says, You needn't be afraid of flying. Please sit. My name is Jason. Sit down, stay.

*

The plane rolls down the runway, gathers speed, takes off and flies. It flies up into the pale, distant sky, breaking through the clouds. The earth below them, an earlier life, are left behind. Jason's hands are dirty and stained with paint. Turning the right one palm up, he holds it out to Stella. Stella puts her left hand in it; his hand is rough and warm. He pulls her hand towards him and puts it in his lap, closes his eyes. Then he falls asleep. Later this will be like an omen. Stella could have figured it out back then – she is afraid, and Jason sleeps. Sleeps even though she is afraid. But he would say he slept so she could see that being afraid was absurd. Back then she didn't understand this.

*

As the plane lands, he opens his eyes and smiles. Such very dark eyes, almost black, with a faraway look. But he is smiling. He says, See, Stella, you made it. He now takes her hand into both of his, and then he kisses her hand, the back of her hand, hard and sure.

Will we see each other again, Stella says. Shall we see each other again.

Yes, Jason says, he says it without thinking it over – Yes.

Stella writes her phone number on his boarding pass. Then she gets up and flees. She climbs out of the plane, down the metal stairs, back to earth without looking back even once.

It is cool, raining. Impossible to know how it will go on from there.

Jason phones three weeks later. Stella never asks him what he did during those three weeks, what he was thinking about for so long; what conclusion he finally arrived at.

One

The house is in a development in the suburbs. It's a simple house, two floors and a mossy, tiled roof, a picture window next to the front door, and a sunroom out the back. The lot isn't a big one. A jasmine hedge secludes it from the street. A tarpaulin has been stretched over the sandpit, and three chairs have already been set up around a garden table standing under a plum tree still bare of leaves. Fragile, yellow flowers in the short grass, maybe winter aconite. At the edge of the garden begins a rank meadow, a fallow field. It's been like that for who knows how long. At some point they'll build new houses there. But so far the garden just runs into the meadow, and stinging nettle and wind grass grow right through the fence.

Stella and Jason's house. This is Stella's and Jason's house;

it's the house Jason buys when Stella is pregnant with Ava. A house for a family. Not a house for always. We'll move from here someday, Jason says. We'll move on.

*

The sunroom smells of soil and wet gravel. An orange blanket is draped over the sofa. Children's books, crayons and a teapot on the little table in front of it; on the rug, a single shoe of Ava's next to a stack of magazines. From the sofa, the view through the windows goes out into the garden and beyond the fence out to the field. The wintry grass is still a dull green. It looks like a body of water. It's as if the wind were reaching with hands into the grass, into the water. Clouds scud by rapidly.

Sometimes when Stella is sitting on the sofa watching Ava in the sandpit – Ava baking a cake out of sand, decorating the cake with shells and gravel, then, calm and direct, not pleading, offering some of the cake to someone whom Stella can't see – she has to suppress an impulse to jump up, snatch Ava out of the sandpit, and flee with her into the house. As if a whirlwind were approaching across the meadow, something formless, something big. Why such a thought?

It's your subconscious, Jason says when she tries to talk to him about it. Just your subconscious, or that of your people, the subconscious of generations.

Just your subconscious.

I don't know if I can follow you, Stella would like to say.

She'd like to say, Maybe it's also a wish? Maybe it's some wild longing.

But that's not how she talks with Jason. Hardly likely.

*

A screen door swings into the kitchen from the sunroom. The kitchen is bright. A stove and a sink under the window; in the middle, a table with four assorted chairs; and above the table, a lamp with a little paper horse suspended from it, twisting in the breeze. Postcards on the silvery refrigerator. A jumble of dishes in a kitchen cabinet on whose doorknob hangs a bunch of dried lavender tied with packing twine. The far wall is painted blue; in front of the blue wall, on top of the chest for their winter boots lies a sheepskin on which Ava sometimes wants to sleep but so far has never managed to fall asleep on. Empty bottles, more magazines in the corner behind the door that leads to the living room; the other door next to it leads to the hall; you can also go into the living room from the hall, and beyond that, into Jason's room or to the front door and outside.

The picture window is in the living room. There's a low armchair in the living room by the window where Stella reads in the evening, not caring that, after it begins to get dark, it's as if she were sitting on a stage. She reads whatever comes to hand, reads everything; she comes across a book, opens it, and dives in. There's something awful about this too. Sometimes Jason says, You'd die if someone were to take the books away from you. Would you die? Stella doesn't answer him. In the middle of the day, between the things to do, to be dealt with, to get behind her, she'll pick up a book and read a page, two pages; it's like breathing; she finds it hard to say what she's just read, and it's really all about something else. About resistance. Or about opposition. Maybe it's about disappearing. It might be.

Stella's books pile up around the armchair. For some time

now Ava's books have also been piling up around the chair. Children's books of thick cardboard.

*

This is the blue door. Let's see who lives there. We'll just knock. Knock!

*

In the hall there's a stairway going up to the first floor. The mail is lying on the bottom step, on the steps above that are Ava's hat, the bicycle keys, chalk, a little plastic horse, a super ball, a broken kaleidoscope, a dinosaur skeleton, and on the top step there's a child's purse embroidered with coloured beads. Fourteen steps, Stella has known this ever since Ava has been learning to count. Upstairs there are three rooms. The master bedroom, a room in the middle for Stella, and Ava's room. There, the night-light in the globe is still on, and a mobile of stars and moons hanging from the ceiling lamp sways in the draught. The bed stands against the wall. Close to the edge of the bed there's a small depression in the tidily smoothed bedspread – Ava was sitting there in the morning while Stella plaited her hair into two stiff little black braids. The stuffed animals lean neatly and importantly against each other, a tiger and a cat, a dishevelled little hedgehog. Ava's stack of memory cards on the red table is distinctly larger than Stella's. A wrinkled princess dress is draped over the rocking chair. On the bookshelf, a series of framed photos that sometimes seems to Stella like a butterfly collection – time impaled, held fast, the extreme and also crazy beauty of single moments. Ava as a baby. Ava with Jason in a boat among the reeds. Ava with matted hair on a chair downstairs in the kitchen, sitting ramrod straight in plaid pyjamas. Ava on Stella's lap, and after her midday nap. And a photo of Stella and Jason by the sea; some day that photo may mean something to Ava: her parents by the sea in the one brief year during which there was no Ava yet. Unimaginable, and at the same time simple.

The door to their bedroom isn't quite closed. Inside, the bed isn't made, the blankets lying one on top of the other, the pillows not fluffed up, the sheet has slipped down. The curtain at the window is still closed; sunlight falls on the floor in a narrow stripe next to Jason's shirt, Stella's book.

In Stella's room her desk stands by the window. A postcard from Clara is propped against a glass vase on the desk. There are also books on the desk, stationery, a ballpoint pen lying diagonally across the line: *My dearest Clara, the morning is so still, so quiet, as if a catastrophe had occurred somewhere, and I go downstairs and open the front door because …* The clock on the windowsill ticks sharply into this stillness. Gift-wrap is spread out on the guest bed, photocopied schedules for Stella's working week, blouses that need to be ironed. The sliding window is open. The wind blows into the stationery, riffling through the sheets of paper.

Three panes of leaded glass are set into the front door, two lilies and one seagull. The panes were a gift from Clara to Stella when she moved in. For Ava's birth. For Stella's wedding, for the move, as a second goodbye. Clara is Stella's best and only friend. Why do you just have only one girlfriend, Ava says. One is quite enough, Jason says then; he says it for Stella, and Stella says, So it would seem.

You can't see either out or in through the leaded glass panes. You can see out only through the little window to the right of the door, out to the garden gate. A wrought-iron gate in a wrought-iron fence. Jason bought the fence along with the house and wanted to rip it out immediately; luckily he hasn't got around to it yet. Stella is glad about the fence. The fence holds quite a few things together here, the garden, the house, the books, Ava and Jason, her life. It isn't as if it would all fly apart without the fence, but Stella considers boundaries important – distance, space for herself. The little window next to the front door is a frame for the view of the fence, the view to the garden gate. You have to put something there, Clara said, a Madonna or something like that; but Stella hasn't found anything yet that could stand there.

*

This is the house on a day in spring.

There's no one there.

Stella is out; she works as a nurse; her patients live in houses in the new development on the other side of the big street.

Jason is also away; he is building a house by a lake.

Ava is at her kindergarten. She's in the blue group; she has a blue flower sewn on her little coat so that she won't forget, and she wears the blue flower like a medal.

The garden gate is of course locked.

The street is empty, no one in sight; the little birds in the hedge make almost no sound.

Two

Three weeks later Stella is at home. Midday, twelve o'clock.

Stella is often at home at twelve in the middle of the day. She has three patients on her weekly schedule: Esther, Julia and Walter. Usually she takes the early shift at Esther's and the daytime shift at Walter's; her shift at Julia's depends on Julia's husband Dermot, on the state of his health; recently his health has been poor. But that particular day Dermot feels able to take Julia to the doctor by himself. And so Stella stays at home. Is able to be home alone in the middle of the day.

The middle of the day in the development is a calm, quiet time. The houses all stand there deserted; their people don't come back till the end of the working day. Stella likes being alone. She's good at busying herself with the garden, her books, the household, the laundry, long telephone conversations with Clara, the newspaper, with doing nothing.

Before, she used to live in the city with Clara in an apartment house on a street with many cafés, bars and nightclubs; people sat on the pavement directly outside their front door at tables under large umbrellas and awnings, and their voices and conversations, their worries, speculations, promises, their exorbitant remarks about happiness and unhappiness resounded in the night all the way up into Stella and Clara's living room. Never. Forever. Ever again, never again, till tomorrow, goodbye. That wasn't so long ago. Stella can't say she misses that life.

Nowadays she likes being alone; before, she didn't like being alone. It's that simple; only she doesn't really know just when this change actually took place. And how – suddenly or gradually? In the course of months, or from one day to the next, from one day that Stella has forgotten to another. It's the same with Clara. Clara lives in a watermill, a thousand kilometres away; she has two children now and is just as addicted to being alone as Stella. That's because of the children, Clara says. They devour you. Stella thinks of that in the mornings when she sits at the kitchen table with Ava, drinking tea with honey and watching her eat a banana.

Clara says you devour us. Is that true, Ava?

Ava's laughter sounds astonished. Indignant and a little as if she'd been caught unawares.

On the days Stella is free until midday, she takes Ava to her kindergarten by bike. Then, cycling home again, she leaves the bike in the front garden, unlocks the front door, enters the hall and feels distinctly grateful, as if everything around her were temporary, as if there were no certainty of permanence.

She couldn't really say how she spends these mornings, these three or four hours. She cleans up the kitchen. She washes her hair. She writes a postcard to Clara, reads a little in the newspaper, reads a book, washes Ava's things, goes through Jason's mail and the bills, tends to the plants in their clay pots on the windowsill, pressing an index finger into the soil around the roots and breaking off the little stems that have finished blooming, just the way Jason always does. Standing at the kitchen window, she looks out at the garden, out towards the meadow, at the formations of dark, luminous clouds far away above the city. Then she brews a pot of tea. Turning on the radio, she listens to a travelogue, then turns the radio off again. She goes upstairs and puts the ironed and folded laundry away in Ava's chest of drawers. Standing in Ava's room, she regards the still life on Ava's table, an apple with a bite taken out of it, a memory card, thin, coloured-pencil shavings, a juice glass. She'd like to clean it up; she'd like it to stay exactly as it is. She has to leave in a quarter of an hour. She has to go. She's got to leave right now.

*

Three days later Stella is home alone in the middle of the day. She's washing the dishes when the doorbell rings. Her teacup, Ava's cup, two plates, a large knife and a small one; at three minutes before twelve Stella is washing a glass. The doorbell rings. She rinses the foam off her hands and reluctantly turns off the tap. Drying her hands on the tea towel, she goes into the hall, looks at herself briefly in the mirror; she'll never forget that at noon that day she was wearing jeans and a wrinkled, grey shirt spattered with water, her hair clasped together in one of Ava's hairslides; she's a bit tired, doesn't want to open the door for anybody, doesn't feel like talking either; she won't forget any of that.

Stella turns the key in the lock, at the same time looking through the window next to the front door out into the garden, towards the fence, to the gate in the fence. Of course the gate is locked. She is about to open the door, but then she carefully removes her hand from the door handle. There's a man she's never seen before standing on the street outside the gate. A young man, maybe thirty, thirty-two years old. Not the postman, not the newspaper boy, not any kind of delivery man, and not the chimney sweep either – a man without any gear, no bag, no backpack, not carrying a bouquet of flowers – a man wearing light-coloured trousers, a dark jacket, no identifiable character-istics. An apparition. His hands are in his trouser pockets. His head is cocked to the side, and he's looking towards the house; looking at the front door, maybe the window next to the front door.

What keeps her from opening the door, walking through the garden towards him and opening the gate, just as she would normally do.

I don't know, Stella will later say to Clara. Can't answer that question. I didn't open the door; I stopped short, recoiled. From what?

The man out on the street waits. Then he takes his right hand out of his pocket and rings again, and suddenly Stella feels – it almost makes her angry – that her heart is speeding up, slowly, steadily, as if her heart understands something that Stella has not yet understood. Without taking her eyes off the stranger, she lifts the receiver of the intercom off the hook on the wall, holds it to her left ear, and says, Yes.

The man outside on the street bends down. Stella has no idea how loud or soft her voice sounds out on the street; she can't recall ever having used the intercom before. He says something into the contraption; she thinks she hears his voice at her ear at the same instant as she hears his voice from the street. The voice at her ear sounds distinctly hoarse. Like the voice of a person who takes pills, who is on medication; no doubt about that. Stella can hear it. She knows all about that.

He says, Hello. We don't know each other. You don't know me. But I know you from having seen you, and I'd like to talk to you. Do you have time.

It isn't a question. Not a real question, and it also sounds rehearsed, something memorised.

Do you have time.

Stella holds the receiver away from her ear. Is this supposed to be a joke? She almost isn't sure that she heard him right. The man outside stands bent over slightly in front of her intercom waiting for an answer. He won't say it again. He won't repeat it; she understood it correctly.

So she holds on tight to the receiver and says loud and clear, I don't have any time. Impossible. Do you understand what I mean? We cannot talk together because I don't have any time at all, none.

Too bad, says the man in front of her house. Oh well then. Maybe another time.

*

He straightens up and looks once more at the front door. Definitely looking at the window behind which, Stella thinks, he can't actually see her but obviously assumes she is standing.

For a moment he stands there expressionless, raising a hand as if in greeting, but maybe it's supposed to be something else. Then he turns and walks away from the fence and towards the street corner.

Stella can no longer see him.

She hangs the receiver back up on the wall and stumbles from the hall into Jason's room. Jason's room is cool and feels a bit abandoned, so very familiar; no connection at all with what caused her to stumble in here. She pushes Jason's chair aside and steps over to the window, unintentionally, carelessly brushing three pens and a piece of paper off the desk, which startles her; she leans forward, looking out into the street; the man has stopped at the street corner, at the edge of their lot, with his back to the house, he stands there. Looks up the street. And down. On the left are houses like this one, on the right, the forest; their street leads to Main Street, the traffic starts at the end of their street. Cars coming from right and left. Other people.

The man on the corner is now rolling himself a cigarette. How about that, it's something he has with him – tobacco. He has tobacco and cigarette papers; he takes these out of his jacket pocket. He's rolling it slowly, carefully, but maybe awkwardly too; maybe he's trembling; hard to tell; Stella in any case is trembling slightly. He lights the cigarette with a lighter and smokes. That goes on for a while. Stella watches him smoking. Time stretches out between them. She thinks she ought to look away, but she can't look away. She sees him, watches him breathe, watches him as he flicks the cigarette to the pavement, puts his hands in his trouser pockets, walks on, down Forest Lane towards Main Street. Until she can't see him any more. Later she'll think, even that was too much.

She steps away from the window and exhales. She picks up the pens and the sheet of paper and puts them back on the desk, pushes the chair back to the desk; Jason's shirt is draped over the back of the chair, and Stella straightens it as if Jason had surprised her at something. Jason's room is so messy. It smells of turpentine, wood and metal, of machine oil, of grass. The computer on the desk is black. The numbers on the weather station on the windowsill flip from 12.19 to 12.20, digital rain clouds approach from the west. The man on the street had looked unemployed, idle, as if he had all the time in the world. He also looked neglected, just a hint of dissipation, just a trace. He had looked like an absolutely free man. So what is so disquieting about that, Stella says out loud; she leaves the room, opens the front door and steps out into the front yard as if she were reclaiming her right to it. How cool it is, delightful and quiet. What is it exactly that is disquieting about a free human being.

*

Stella leaves the house at a quarter past one. She pushes her bicycle out into the street, pulls the gate shut behind her, stands for a while looking at her house from the outside. She's standing where the stranger stood. She looks at her front door, at the narrow window next to the front door. She was standing behind that window, and he knew it.

What is there to see?

A brick house with a mossy tile roof. A front door with leaded glass panes set into it, to the left a wooden bench, next to the bench a little olive tree in a clay pot, and under the bench, Ava's rubber boots. Stella has no idea how they got there, how long they've been there. To the right of the front door, the picture window; clearly visible through it, the armchair with a crumpled blanket draped over the armrest, piles of books, and on the wide windowsill, pillows, a stuffed zebra, a tea glass, a bottle of water, and something small that Stella thinks might be Jason's glasses case. You can see all of it; for a moment she is stunned at this exhibition of private things, at her carelessness. The stranger on the street was able to see all that, and she'd allowed it; she's the one who made it possible, after all. What is it really – recklessness?

She gets on her bike and turns left into Forest Lane. Crossing Main Street at the big intersection, she loses the stranger's trail, if there even was one. She rides past the shopping centre, across the car park with the shopping centre's flapping banners and clanking flag chains, a wild noise that Ava loves. She turns into the new development. Large, free-standing one-family houses, with families sitting on the terraces as if posed there, defying the chilly May wind. Dogs throw themselves against garden gates and are generously whistled back. Stella rides down Pine Lane, Stone Pine Lane and Fir Tree Lane to the middle of the development. She takes this route every day. Ava's kindergarten, a park and the office of the nursing station in the Community Centre are all located in the middle of the development. She isn't paying attention. Not concentrating, isn't being careful. She's glad when she can park the bike in front of the Community Centre. The door is wide open; a breeze is blowing through the foyer where small reading lamps are lit on little tables at which no one ever sits. Stella often arrives at the office half an hour before her shift starts; she almost always has a cup of coffee with Paloma. Paloma is fifty, tall and gaunt; her expression is disdainful and at the same time melancholy. Occasionally she baby-sits for Ava; she's curious but not too curious; there are days when Stella discusses Ava with Paloma; sometimes they talk about Jason too, and if not about Jason, then occasionally about Stella's dreams, about her uneasiness that could be caused by the weather or something else. Paloma has a penchant for Swedish crime novels. She almost always wears black dresses and ethnic necklaces. She looks like an actress in a silent film, but maybe, Stella thinks, that's because Paloma is often on the phone while handing out keys, pushing weekly schedules across her desk, and making signals with her hands and eyes, signals that Stella could interpret one way or another or yet in some completely different way. This afternoon Paloma is on the phone to her mother, maybe to her mother. She is often interrupted by the other person; this is unusual, and her voice alternates between annoyance and forbearance.

Yes. No. I can't keep telling you the same thing all the time. You don't challenge yourself enough. You have to move around more, you have to change your habits. Put on a hat and go outside.

Stella steps behind the desk, takes Esther's key off the hook, signs the week's schedule, which is already full of scrawled notes of changes and substitutions. She would like to wait till Paloma finishes her conversation. She would like to say to Paloma, Just imagine, a stranger rang our doorbell today. He said he'd like to speak to me, but I don't know him at all. I've never seen him before.

How would that sound?

It wouldn't sound normal.

But still, she could say it that way, blush and then laugh about it, and maybe with the laugh this unpleasant feeling would go away – uneasiness, anxiety, as if she had overlooked something. She steps to the front of the desk.

Just for once, stick to the arrangement, Paloma is saying. She holds the receiver away from her ear, and putting her hand over the mouthpiece and rolling her eyes up towards the ceiling, she whispers, Good Lord.

Till later, Stella mouths soundlessly. She points at the clock, holds out four fingers. She leaves the office, passing the empty tables, the display cases in which there are pictures by the schoolchildren held in place by colourful magnets: giant suns, smiling flowers, children from all the continents holding hands. She says hello to the janitor. She buttons up her rain jacket, walks out of the foyer.

*

Esther is eighty-two years old. She isn't Stella's favourite patient, but not unbearable either. It's best not to have favourites among the patients. Even so, Stella likes Dermot best, Julia's husband. Esther is lying in bed. Actually, she still gets up every afternoon and walks from her bedroom into the living room or the kitchen. But for the last few weeks she's just wanted to lie in bed, dozing, maybe eat a piece of buttered toast with a little orange marmalade, drink some tea with it, and have Stella open the window every two minutes and then close it again. Not in a good mood today, the carer doing the night shift had written into the record book. Esther's bedroom is small. Her bed stands in front of a wall of bookshelves; when Esther lies on her side she'll grab a book from the shelf at random, open it, read a sentence aloud, shake her head at what she's read and drop the book behind the bed. The little night table is full of medications, pill dispensers, water glasses, various watches, glasses, thermometers and first-aid kits. Esther's skin is parchment-thin and wrinkled; it tears like paper. The room smells of old age and illness, but of something else too. Of incense and myrrh, Esther's cigars, dusty books, and the flowers on which Esther insists and which stand around in large glass vases. The window is open, the radio is on, with a lackadaisical, sleepy lecture that sounds like a lot of drivel to Stella, about something imaginary, a lot of drivel from the world of shadows. Now finally, in taking care of Esther, she emerges from those other thoughts into the familiar rhythm of touching, sick-room procedures, responsibilities, the counting of drops, emptying of tubes, pots, pails, Esther's spit cup, the glass for her teeth, the bowl for the warm soapy water. Don't be so lazy, Esther, try to help a little. And Esther pulls herself up by means of the handle that's part of the apparatus rigged up over her bed, sitting up and dangling her legs over the edge of the bed with the same expression Ava sometimes has, sullen, restrained, pretending to be far away.

Esther says, My feet are cold, please close the window; turn off the radio now; put on my socks; I want those soft socks Ricarda knits for me. Ricarda is Esther's daughter, and Stella can't remember any more when she last saw her here. Esther's eyeballs are red-veined; the irises are a bright, profound blue. Seven drops into the left eye, seven drops into the right. Her blood pressure has dropped through the floor. Last night, though, it was one hundred and eighty. What caused that, Esther? Sometimes they can joke with each other, find a common language, common ground, two people forced to touch each other, to handle each other, to share information. It could just as well be the other way around. It could be Esther who swaddles Stella. The present arrangement is a coincidence, nothing more. Do you have a fever? Come, Esther, lift up your arm and hold the thermometer. You feel quite hot.

Esther says, Nonsense.

Stella squeezes a drop of blood from her earlobe, measures the blood sugar level, enters Esther's catastrophic numbers on the chart in the record book, as if they weren't catastrophic. She calculates and counts out drops and pills, and all that time Esther keeps talking to herself, jumping from one subject to another, from a long-ago year into the here and now, from a suspicion to a fragile memory, from the memory to the stubborn pain flaring up in her back or in her eyes or in her chest, her knee, the joints of her fingers, her head, her behind, her back.

Don't be so rough, Stella. What are you thinking of? Don't keep frowning all the time. You'll look like an angry parrot when you get old.

Esther giggles.

Stella washes Esther's face. She washes Esther's hands, her back, her armpits, her private parts. Esther's feet; Esther is very proud of her feet; they're the only part of her body that seem unscathed, the slender feet of a dancer.

Are you hungry?

No.

Esther doesn't want to eat anything, but she claims that the bread for toast is all gone; Stella should go shopping; Stella finds enough toasting bread in Esther's kitchen to last for months, goes shopping anyway. In the supermarket she stands leaning against the newspaper rack, reading the week's horoscope; she's tired; the in-store music has something sad about it. To Stella it seems as if the lights were being turned out in slow motion.

Esther is asleep when she gets back. Or pretends to be asleep, and Stella quietly closes the curtain, does the rest of her work. She cleans the bathroom and the kitchen, straightens the living room table, stacks the entire spring's newspapers, one on top of the other; she looks to see what Esther has marked in the television listings, the programmes she wants to watch or might watch: a travelogue about Mongolia, a political round table, a concert in Venice, an evening's discussion of mortality. Stella puts some orange marmalade on a piece of buttered toast and cuts it into tiny squares; she makes coffee, puts the bread and coffee by Esther's bed and sits down for a while on the chair next to it. She sits next to Esther's bed the way she sometimes sits next to Ava's bed. The hands of the large clock on the wall above the bookshelf drop, stand still and drop again.

I'm leaving, Esther, Stella says. The night shift will be here at eight. Take care of yourself; be sensible.

Esther doesn't reply.

In the record book Stella writes: Sleeping; pretends to be sleeping. In the hall she puts on her rain jacket and closes the front door behind her. Bicycling back to the Community Centre, she signs out on the weekly schedule, and hangs Esther's key back up on the board behind Paloma's desk. Paloma has already left; she leaves her office so tidy every day that it looks as if she weren't ever coming back. The lobby is deserted; the ferns in the big buckets stand motionless as if before an explosion. The idyll of the children's pictures in the glass case looks suddenly ugly and slightly suspect. At the far end of the hall the janitor is on his knees in the twilight, fiddling with an electric outlet.

Good evening.

Same to you.

The entrance door stands wide open; outside, the real world.

*

Stella picks up Ava from kindergarten.

She can finally pick Ava up from kindergarten. In the cloak-room Stella takes off Ava's slippers and puts on her street shoes. Ava can do all this by herself already; she's four, going on five. But at the end of a long day in kindergarten she's so tired that she forgets her independence and holds out her legs to Stella, little fat legs in tights put on backwards. Stella is grateful. Ava isn't the last child to be picked up. There are six or seven other kids there; their jackets still hanging on the clothes' hooks; little pictures of tractors, flowers and butterflies are pasted next to the hooks. A snail is pasted next to Ava's hook, which she has been and continues to be distressed about since her first day in kindergarten. Ava has the same black hair and eyes as Jason. She's a loner and just as stubborn as Jason. She's affectionate and impatient. Maybe as impatient as Stella. The teachers had asked Stella whether she reaffirms Ava sufficiently. Stella had a hard time understanding the question. Whether she reaffirms Ava sufficiently? She reaffirms Ava from morning to night. Sometimes she's afraid she reaffirms her too much. Why the question? Because Ava lacks confidence. Because she holds back, because she doesn't dash off right away, doesn't want to recite any poems and doesn't want to stand in the middle during their morning circle. Because she doesn't want to dress up for the carnival, because she only wants to dress up at home. All these things are part of a pattern; the teachers observe Ava carefully. I reaffirm Ava, Stella said; of course I do. She takes Ava's round face in her hands and kisses her on both cheeks. Ava. Avenka. How was your day.

Rabbits can have shaggy fur, Ava says. Like dogs. They can be as shaggy as a dog, did you know that, and she slides off the bench dragging her jacket behind her; she says, Put out the light, Mama, you shouldn't forget to put out the light. Why do I have to tell you that over and over again.

Stella switches the light off in the cloakroom. She says to Ava, And you should wave to them, and together they wave to the teachers sitting with the last of the children at the round table outside on the lawn. The children have put their heads down on the tabletop. The inevitable pot of peppermint tea stands on the table, coloured plastic cups next to it. Stella thinks she knows what the tea smells like and how it tastes. She buckles Ava into the child's seat on the bicycle and pedals out of the courtyard. The paths through the park are so green that they seem almost dark, and out of the thicket at the edge of the path come peacocks heavily dragging their long feather trains through the sand.

*

Stella and Ava cycle home. Through the new development, along Fir Tree, Stone Pine and Pine Tree Lanes, past the shopping centre, across Main Street and into the old development where a few cars are now parked in front of the houses and the front doors are open; it smells of lilac, charcoal grills and lighter fluid, of neighbourhood. Stella unlocks the gate, pushes the bike into the garden, lifts Ava out of the child seat, and hears the gate close behind her; she listens for the solid sound of the lock snapping shut.

What are we having to eat today?

Pancakes. With apple sauce and cinnamon and sugar.

I'm going to eat seven, Ava says. Seven pancakes. Definitely.

*

Stella washes her hands at the kitchen sink. She listens to the telephone answering machine – a message for Jason, one from Paloma about the week's schedule, and Clara's voice, relaxed and pleasant: Stella, call me back; I'm thinking of you. Is everything all right?

Stella opens the door to the sunroom all the way. She turns on the radio, empties the washing machine, prepares the pancake batter, sings along with the radio, drinks tea in the basket chair in the garden and watches Ava in the sandpit making spirals with shells; she listens to Ava's conversations with herself. Questions, counting rhymes, whispered riddles. *Tomorrow morning I'll get the queen's child.*

The evening is cool, the humidity moving into the garden from the field, almost palpable. They eat in the kitchen at the table, sitting across from each other, Ava and Stella under the lamp in the company of the radio voices, the alternation of reports on war, climate catastrophes and jazz.

Don't take so much sugar, Stella says; better if you take more apple sauce.

I'll never eat in kindergarten again, Ava says; I'm not going to ever eat anything there. If I ever, one single time, eat something at the kindergarten again, I'm going to throw up. She gives Stella a long, searching look. Stella endures it, doesn't comment. Ava eats five pancakes. She says, There's a boy in my group, his name is Stevie. Then she gets up, walks around the table, sits down in Stella's lap, and wraps her arms tightly around Stella's neck.

*

Outside the sky turns dark blue and black at the edges. Lights go on in the house next door and in the house across the street. Ava's bath mixture smells of peach and melon; her quilt rustles, her pyjamas are soft as moleskin. Stella puts Ava to bed, she reads to her, sings to her. *The pear tree sways, it sways as in a dream.* Stella thinks that she ought to see to it that Ava is more self-assured as she's going to sleep, to see to it that Ava is more self-confident at the end of her day. She ought to be more pragmatic, the way she is with Esther, Julia, Walter; she ought to close the door to Ava's room behind her with pragmatic authority and call out in a firm voice, Good night! Sleep well now. Go to sleep! But she finds it hard to do. The room is safe still, and the globe glows; the Atlantic glows. But the night is the more defined, it is the greater constant. Ava doesn't know that, Stella thinks that *she* knows it. *Tomorrow morning, if God will.*

When is Papa coming back, Ava says. Maybe she does know after all.

In three days, Stella says. Three more sleeps, then Papa will come back.

Three

Next day the stranger comes again, at the same time. He apparently knows when Stella is at home, and when she's home alone. Stella is in the kitchen looking in the cabinet under the sink for the brush for Ava's shoes when the doorbell rings, and even though she hadn't been thinking of him at all, even though she never assumed that he would come back so soon – even though she had actually forgotten him, he immediately comes to mind again. She knows who's ringing the bell. She knows that it's not the postman, not a messenger, not her neighbour, not a child in need of a bicycle pump, unfortunately not the chimney sweep, and not the man from the gas company. She puts the little suitcase in which Jason keeps the shoe polish things down in front of the sink, and straightens up. Her knee joints crack as she stands up, and for a moment she feels dizzy. She goes out of the kitchen down the hall to the front door. Looking out of the window she takes hold of the intercom receiver; she says, Yes.

Yes, as she looks at the stranger standing on the street outside her garden gate in the same clothes he was wearing yesterday, his hands in his jacket pockets, and, as far as she can see at this distance, the same totally expressionless face as yesterday. She can't really see his face, but his aura is expressionless, and the way he now leans down to the intercom, not taking his hands out of his jacket pockets nor looking in her direction, but rather keeping his face turned towards the pavement – his manner is so flat and toneless that it gives Stella the chills.

Hello. It's me. I wanted to ask if maybe today you have time for a conversation.

No, Stella says. She feels her knees trembling; she is surprised at how quickly that can happen. Is she really trembling again? It's true. She is trembling.

She says, No, I don't. I don't have time today. And tomorrow I won't have any time either; on the whole, I don't have any time. I'm sorry, excuse me.

The man outside on the street says, You really don't have to excuse yourself. You really don't need to do that. He stands there still leaning forward as he says it, looking at the grass between the paving stones. He coughs.

Stella hangs up the receiver.

This he seems to understand, he straightens up stretching a little; it almost looks as if he were yawning.

You really don't need to do that. What is it that makes this remark such an impertinence? Why is this remark an effrontery behind which something else seems to be concealed. The word 'threat' comes to Stella's mind like a warning. Her mouth is dry and her heart barely beating. She sees the stranger walk to the corner of the street. From Jason's window she watches him smoking; she wishes he would turn around, just once, turn around and look towards Jason's room, and she hisses it: Turn around. But clearly the stranger is the stronger one. He smokes, as deliberately as yesterday; then he flicks the finished cigarette onto the pavement and walks off.

*

Later, Stella can't remember any more whether she didn't say, after all, that she knew what she needed to do and what not. Did she say it? I know what I need to do and what I don't, and then hung the receiver back up? Or did she only think it. Wasn't she quick or aggressive enough to say it out loud? She cannot remember. But she remembers clearly the feeling of humiliation and her decision to let this be the last time she ever talks to that man. Not even to go to the door from now on when the bell rings. Going to the door twice was enough; there will be no third time, and it remains to be seen if he'll even ring a third time.

*

That evening she locks the front door from the inside.

Waiting till Ava is asleep, she takes the telephone to the kitchen, but then changes her mind; she doesn't call Jason after all. She sits at the table in the kitchen, reading the paper and drinking a beer she's taken from the refrigerator; she reads a story about Calcutta and another one about Siberia and then something else. She looks up between the lines and sees herself from outside, from a point outside the house, a corner of the garden perhaps, from the fence, the high grass in the uncultivated meadow. She sees a woman sitting alone at a table under a lamp, reading.

*

That's me, Stella thinks. That's me. Stella.

Four

Next morning the bell rings shortly before ten, and it rings as if it were a certainty that Stella wouldn't come to the door. Casually, in passing. Much more briefly than yesterday or the day before yesterday. The ringing of someone who just wants to say, Here I am, I'm here, standing outside your door.

Stella sees him. She's sitting upstairs in her room at her desk, and she sees him. She's been sitting in her room at her desk by the window and waiting since returning home after taking Ava to kindergarten – the shift at Esther's begins in an hour and a half. She saw him coming. He was coming from the left. Not from the direction of Main Street, from the shopping centre, from the bus route from the new development; he's coming from the left, from her own neighbourhood. Appearing at the

edge of her property, he walks at once both listlessly and pur-
posefully along the fence, stops in front of the garden gate, turns
and rings the bell, and almost simultaneously puts a hand into
the inside pocket of the same old jacket and takes out something white, an envelope.

He lets the envelope drop into the mailbox attached to the
fence and looks up towards Stella's room. Then he crosses the
street, turns into Forest Lane, heads down towards Main Street
and disappears.

*

For a while Stella sits at her desk, leaning back, hands folded
in her lap. A flock of sparrows flies up out of the trees in the
garden across the way, as if hurled into the air by a large hand.
Downstairs in the kitchen the gas hot water heater switches on
and off again. Four minutes, five. Then she stands up.

The air in the garden outside is wonderful. It smells of late
spring, sweet woodruff and boxwood. Postponing it is out of the
question. Stella opens the mailbox and the white envelope drops
into her hand like something that can't be changed any more.

The envelope is of ordinary paper, precisely addressed.
Stella's first and last name, house number, street and postal
code properly provided in a curving, feminine handwriting, a
postage stamp, as if the sender had intended to have the post
office deliver the letter, only to change his mind at the last
moment. The stamp is neutral, inconspicuous, the head of
a queen on a green background. Stella turns the letter over.
It seems there's nothing to hide; on the back are the sender's
name, house number, street and postal code written in the same
matter-of-fact hand:

Mister Pfister.

Mister Pfister is the sender of the letter, and he lives, as Stella now reads, on the same street as she does. Seven or eight houses farther on; they are neighbours. It makes no sense to take a letter to the post office if you can deliver it yourself. Mr Pfister simply drops a letter like this into the mailbox personally; that's no problem for him.

Stella doesn't know her neighbours. People around here are extremely reserved; they make no effort to get to know each other. A female university student lives in the house next door with changing subtenants. In the house next to her, an Asian family with half-grown children; in the house across the way, a retired teacher; that's as far as Stella has got. Mister Pfister's being a neighbour narrows the radius from one moment to the next. She thought he would simply vanish again. She didn't think that he was this close, had been all along, only a few houses farther on; that he lived here – just like her.

Stella sits down with the letter on the bench next to the front door. The outside thermometer says fourteen degrees centigrade, and the little olive tree ought to be watered; it stands just under the gutter and seldom gets any rain. A shiny blackbird comes hopping across the grass along the hedge. Stella crosses her legs, puts the letter down next to her on the bench.

Then she opens it. She tears it open. She picks it up and rips it open. The feeling she had only the day before yesterday – the quiet amazement, the memory of what it was like once to be tempted – is totally gone.

*

By evening the next day Jason is back. He puts Ava to bed

while Stella cleans up in the kitchen; she can hear Ava jumping upstairs. Jason was away for a week. Ava is exuberant.

It's nice when Jason comes back. And in a certain way also nice when he goes away again.

Jason builds houses. Restaurants, hotels, workshops, apartment houses, pavilions, factories, bungalows. Sometimes Stella thinks that maybe he really wanted to do something else. She couldn't say why she thinks that; she can sense a certain disillusionment in the way Jason deals with his work, his reluctance to talk about it; she is glad that she doesn't have to sense this disillusionment every day. She herself is not disillusioned about his work. He was already doing this work when she put her hand in his on the airplane as it took off; the dirt on his hand wasn't from working as a sculptor but from laying tiles; and Stella claims that she knew that. Sometimes Jason draws a cat for Ava, a cottage with a smoking chimney, and also a big bee; sometimes he draws Ava with braids sitting at the kitchen table early in the morning in front of a bowl of porridge. Drawings that frighten and delight Ava; but Jason is hiding something, it's in the way he then takes the drawings away from Ava. Probably, Stella thinks, Jason feels that he missed out on something. He hides the drawings in the waste-paper bin, and she retrieves them from the waste-paper bin and saves them for Ava. Jason earns enough money with his work, money for this house, for Stella and Ava, and the work distracts him and tires him. Without his work he would feel worse. Jason is calm only when he is tired. Back then, on the airplane, he was. So tired that he fell asleep before the plane had flown through the clouds. Otherwise he might not even have got involved with Stella. None of all they had here would have come to be. None of it, not even the glass of water on the table, and certainly not Ava's little voice upstairs in the house.

*

Did I let go of your hand on the plane when I was sleeping?
    No, you didn't let go of my hand. I could feel that you were asleep; you twitched in your sleep; you were dreaming. I could tell you were dreaming.
    They keep asking each other. The same question, the same answer. As if to hold on to the beginning, to keep reaffirming it.

*

Stella puts Jason's clothes into the washing machine, his black work trousers, the blue overalls, the green shirts. Coins in the trouser pockets, a pencil, a pebble. Jason brought back a piece of wood for Ava with an ingrown pine cone; he brought her a booklet full of glittering decals. The piece of wood and the book are lying on the kitchen table, like proof of his return. Stella puts on her jacket, unfolds the second chair on the terrace, and turns off the light in the sunroom. This year the hornets simply moved from one corner of the shed to the other; when the light in the sunroom is turned on, they leave their nest, flying in the darkness across the lawn, bumping against the glass panes, and falling stunned onto the windowsill. Jason comes out on the terrace with two bottles of beer; he stops briefly and looks around as if to make sure where he actually is. Then he sits down next to Stella.
    You look tired, he says. Ava says you should come upstairs again. To say goodnight and bring her something to drink.
    In a little while, Stella says.

They sit next to each other looking out across the garden, to the wild meadow; skylarks swoop diagonally down into the grass, the nocturnal sky is lilac-coloured. Jason stretches and exhales. He opens the two beers with his lighter and says, Jesus. I have four days, maybe five; then I have to leave again. There's something I'm doing wrong, and someday we'll do something else, Stella; we can't stay here like this forever.

When Ava has to start school, Stella says. She says, By then at the latest, a year and a half to go still.

Jason says, A year and a half. Do you know how long that is? You've got to come and see me at the construction site next weekend; you have to plan to do that, and you should make a note of it on the weekly schedule before someone else wants to take that time off. The first storey is done. The roof isn't on yet; the stairway just reaches up into the sky. They've now decided on the materials to be used; they want the doors made of rusty metal. What do you think of that. Metal from barn doors; they want to see the traces of other people's work when they sit down evenings by the fireplace.

Stella would like to stay with the image of the metal from barn doors; it's a picture she could spend some time on, but she can't stand it any longer. She takes Mister Pfister's letter out of her jacket pocket; she wants to get it over with. She's got to get it over with. She thought about not telling Jason about Mister Pfister's letter. She thought about it pretty intensely. But she knows it's better to tell Jason how matters stand than to let him find out on his own. If Jason were to find out on his own it might lead to misunderstandings. To a fight.

And Mister Pfister is an unpredictable factor. Hard to say what might happen next.

Jason takes the letter, even that is a relief. He looks at Stella, takes the envelope from her hand, takes out the letter, awkwardly unfolds it and reads.

I wish you would look at me.
That you would look at me and listen to me. I also wish that
we had always known each other; you're getting older, and
we don't have much time left. You'll smile when you look at
me; it can't be any other way. I'll show you what I see: the
thrush, her spotted feathers, the park, pages of the book I'm
reading.

Good lord, Jason says. What is this? He reads the letter all the way to the end, folds it up again, and puts it back into the envelope. He looks at the envelope, both sides; puts it on the table in front of him, then he leans back. The expression on his face is really quite inscrutable. He says, OK. And what's that supposed to mean?

Stella says, I have no idea. She thinks her voice sounds false, even though she's trying to tell the truth. She says, I have no idea; I don't know him. I've never seen him before. On Wednesday he stood outside the door for the first time and wanted – to talk to me.

He wanted what? Jason says; now he's looking at Stella.

To talk to me, Stella says irritably. I can only repeat what he said. He said he would like to talk to me, and I said I had no time to have a conversation.

He was standing outside our front door, Jason says. He says, Is that right?

He puts the bottle of beer down on the table without looking at it, and Stella realises that he can't bring himself to stop looking at her face, that he doesn't trust her. Jason thinks she would show her true face only the moment his eyes are turned elsewhere. She feels something electric between herself and him, something, surprisingly, from before, from their first months – fear and uncertainty, doubt about the feelings of the other, of one's own feelings. Jason looks at her as if maybe he didn't know her at all, as if he were discovering at precisely this moment, after five years and seven months, that Stella isn't the person he thought she was. He looks as if he wanted to get up and leave, and Stella suddenly remembers an evening five years ago, an evening in the hallway of the apartment where they were living at the time, when Jason, drunk, banged his head against the apartment door, over and over again, because he wanted to leave and couldn't leave. Her recollection of it is unexpected and it is frightening, and Stella leans forward and takes Jason's hand.

She says, No, he wasn't standing outside the front door. He was standing outside the garden gate, and I spoke to him through the intercom. She says, He came again on Thursday, and again yesterday. Yesterday he dropped this letter in the mailbox, and today I'm showing it to you.

Jason says, And you have no idea. You have no idea, but you're certain that you don't know him. Never saw him before.

I'm sure I don't know him. I've never seen him before.

Jason pulls his hand from hers. He says, Shit.

You can say that again, Stella says.

*

Later, the light of dawn wakes her up. It's five o'clock in the

morning. Beside her Jason is asleep, lying on his back, his arms
stretched out, relaxed. She wakes up because it's unusual for
him to be there, lying next to her and reaching for her in his
sleep. She lies awake next to Jason and thinks that Mister Pfister's sentences, his words, that for her don't really fit together –
each word standing alone by itself is a foreign word and toneless
– apply to her and Jason in a spooky way. She wishes that Jason
would look at her. She wishes that he would listen to her. She
wants to show him what she sees. She wishes she could always
have known Jason, although she knows that if she had always
known Jason, she would certainly not still be with him today.
She has got older. Jason has got older. Ava is growing up.

*

Noiselessly Stella goes to Ava's room; she flips Ava's sleep-
warmed blanket over. She goes into her room and stands by the
window for a while; when Ava was a baby, she used to stand by
this window too, in the evenings, with Ava in her arms, and at
night, after nursing her, she would stand here by herself. The
waxing moon is setting over the house across the street. No
birdsong yet. Stella can hear Ava and Jason breathing.

Five

Jason stays four days. He takes Ava to kindergarten and picks her up from there.

*

Jason is here, isn't he, Paloma says as Stella comes into the office. She says it casually, pleasantly, not necessarily to embarrass Stella.

Yes, Jason is here, Stella says. He's – how would you say – onshore?

And Paloma smiles and prudently says nothing.

*

The days have turned unexpectedly warm, and the hedges and

trees have suddenly burst into white bloom, hastily, as if belat-edly. After work Stella rides home on her bike, sees Jason's car in the driveway and cycles past the house and farther on, along the edge of the forest until there are only fields on both sides of the road. Rabbits crouch in the ditches so motionless that Stella can look into their blank eyes. She cycles straight ahead until she comes to an invisible boundary; she couldn't say why she turns around there and cycles back, but at some point she turns around. She thinks, tomorrow I'll ride farther, but she doesn't ride any farther. On the second afternoon she goes to the movies and sees a film that takes place in San Francisco: American light, middle-aged women who, after running, support themselves on park benches to tie their trainers more tightly, who turn their possibly make-up-free faces to the camera with an expression that seems docile and idiotic to Stella, a stubborn faith in better times ahead. Stella used to like going to the movies alone in the afternoon, but ever since Ava came along, she can no longer forget about reality unless the cinema is totally dark. She sees the exit sign in the left-hand corner of the theatre glowing throughout the entire film; she has to go to the toilet and can't think of anything else. As she comes out of the cinema, the day outside is still bright. She pushes her bike through the pedes-trian zone; she is hungry, thinks vaguely about not wanting to work as a nurse any more, taking a trip, having her hair cut; she thinks of nothing at all as she pushes her bike home through the pedestrian zone.

*

Paloma stops by in the evening. She brings tulips and ranuncu-lus, a bottle of wine, and a game for Ava in which she can fish little cardboard fishes out of a golden box with a fishing rod. She brings films, banana gummies and candyfloss in a plastic container. Goodbye, till later. Ava forgets Stella, forgets Jason. She waves to them from the kitchen table, casually and without looking up. It's the golden box and the candyfloss, but it's also Paloma's way of speaking to Ava, looking at her for a long time, thoughtfully and candidly.

Take care, Paloma says to Stella and Jason. She stands by the open door, her arms crossed over her chest; then she disappears into the house.

*

Right or left, Jason says. Stella knows that Jason is really asking himself and that he would drive in exactly the opposite direction she would like anyway. Automatically. A reflex; she could think about what this reflex actually meant, but she has the feeling that she wouldn't arrive at any conclusion. She thinks, Right, and they drive in the car along the dark forest in the direction of Main Street. Let's turn left and drive along the lakeshore, Jason says. Let's see what we'll find.

There are impressive rain clouds above the tile roofs of the new development. Traffic is sluggish; Stella says, almost casually, Can you turn off the radio; she rolls down the window and sticks her hand out. They drive out of the city, along the shore of the lake, across the bridge to the other side and up into the hills. Jason parks at the observation platform, and they get out and walk down towards the valley; they share a beer on a bench with a view of the water. We're sitting next to each other the way we were on the airplane, Stella thinks, and she wonders about the silence between them that seems to be closed and taken for granted. Jason, in any case, is a taciturn man. But maybe the silence is cryptic, expectant; perhaps Jason is being watchful. Is Stella watchful?

On the other side of the lake, some late rockets soar up above the trees. Fountains of cool blue and silver sparks shoot up and spread out, opening up like flowers or stars. The explosions sound faint, and it is starting to rain. They continue to sit there until the rain starts to come down through the dense foliage of the May-time trees, then Jason gets to his feet, pulling Stella up from the bench. They walk back to the car; Stella's face is wet, and she is suddenly awake and exuberant, and happy. She turns to Jason and holds him tight, even though she knows that it will make him suspicious.

Get in, Jason says. Not fending her off, more likely embarrassed. Get in, let's drive a bit farther, and Stella regretfully pulls the car door shut.

She thinks, Well, so that's how it is then. Doesn't matter; it doesn't matter. That's how it is then.

How is Esther doing, Jason says. What's Walter doing; what has Dermot got to say; he starts the engine, turns the car around and rolls back down to the street. For Jason it's easiest to ask questions and talk while he's driving a car. Having a conversation with him while sitting across from each other at a table, perhaps eating, drinking, is almost impossible. While driving he can look at the street, he's busy, it's easier for him then; the street is a red thread that leads through the imponderable, seemingly mined territory of a conversation. Stella thinks she knows this, and it makes her both inattentive and relaxed. She gazes out the window, turns back to look at the lake; the surface of the water is choppy and metallic; a last rocket shoots up over the trees.

She says, I have to stop, Jason. I have to stop working for Paloma. I have to get away from Walter and Dermot. She says, Thanks for asking what Dermot says; because Julia doesn't say anything at all any more. Julia sits in a chair by the window twiddling her thumbs all day long.

Jason says nothing, and Stella is silent for a while, then she says, Maybe I'd like to sit at a cash register in the shopping centre. I'd like to sell coffee and croissants there in that little booth. For one season I'd like to pick strawberries. Train as a florist. Help out in a bookshop. Sit around in an office like Paloma. Maybe I'd like to be Paloma?

It occurs to Stella that it might be risky to talk to Jason about her ideas of another life, a different profession. What is he supposed to say? But he's laughing softly now and he says, Then just go ahead and do it. Not being Paloma, but everything else – why don't you simply do it.

Because it isn't simple, Stella says. At any rate, for me it's not simple. Nothing in this world seems to be simple to me, except maybe preparing supper for Ava or putting fresh sheets on the beds or washing the dishes properly.

Jason nods. He turns on the windscreen wipers; the road is a dark green ribbon being rolled out before them, silky, wide. The rain blurs the beechwoods; the trees seem to fall into one another. It's warm inside the car. Jason takes his right hand off the steering wheel to rub his head; putting his hand back on the steering wheel, letting it drop back on the steering wheel, he says, By the way, I walked by there.

Where did you walk by, Stella says; her stomach contracts, her heart suddenly pounds faster as if it had been waiting for this sentence, as if the sentence were a hideous cue.

Mister Pfister, Jason says. He pronounces the name in a funny way, something between hostile and revolted. I walked by Mister Pfister's house; I had a look at it.

And…, Stella says.

Were you ever there, Jason says.

No, Stella says truthfully; no, I never was.

She'd thought about going past Mister Pfister's house. Not in the days since Jason's been home, but the day before Jason came back, on Friday. She thought about it, and she didn't go by there; she didn't want to look at it after all. What was there actually to see, and what for.

She says firmly, I don't want to see it. I never go down the street in that direction, and I'm not going to do it now either.

Yes, Jason says, but he says it as if it weren't about Stella but about himself and this was something completely different. I know. But I went down there and looked at it; it's a totally normal house, exactly the same as ours. It doesn't look either occupied or unoccupied. Anyway, he seems to live there alone; it has only his name on the door, and he wasn't there. In case you were going to ask.

I would have wanted to ask that, Stella says. Of course I would have wanted to ask that. I would have asked you whether you'd seen him.

No, I didn't see him, Jason says. He looks into the rear-view mirror as if something were approaching very fast, but the road behind them is empty.

He says, I don't think he was there. For some reason I don't think he was home.

Did you walk by or stop in front of it.

I stopped in front of it.

For how long, Stella says; she can't help smiling.

Long enough, Jason says. Long enough in any case.

*

Back home, Paloma is sitting in Stella's easy chair by the window watching television. She's drawn her feet up onto the chair; she doesn't look out as the car drives up. Jason gets out and opens the gate. Stella stays in the car; she sees Paloma through the windscreen, framed by the picture window like a painting – Paloma's dependable figure in the flickering glow of the TV; she watches as Paloma casually takes a large swallow from her glass of water and puts the glass back on the table without taking her eyes away from what's happening on the TV. For one moment Stella has a tremendous and simple longing for Clara. What would Clara do? She would be sitting in the kitchen and would certainly be eating something, a ham sandwich with mustard and pickles probably; the radio station would have been turned from classical music to pop; she'd have lit candles; she'd probably be drunk, and Ava would still be awake. In spite of that it's a gift for Stella to have Paloma sitting in the armchair by the window. Taking Stella's place for a short, maybe an important time.

Gifts like this, Stella thinks, are something new in my life. Didn't exist before this. Or I didn't recognise them?

*

The next day Jason takes Ava to kindergarten, comes back, packs his own suitcase, and is ready to drive off. He stands next to Stella in the garden watching as, her hands in yellow plastic gloves, she pulls the wind grass out of the rose bed, pulls dandelions up by the roots, stinging nettle, wild oats. The sunshine is incredibly bright. Stella sees her shadow, Jason's shadow, and the distance between them.

She says, Did Ava cry. She can't look at Jason.

No, Jason says. She didn't cry. I think she'll cry this evening. Will you call me.

We'll call you, Stella says. She does get up after all and embraces Jason fiercely, exuberantly; then she lets him go.

What are you going to do about Mis-ter-pfis-ter, Jason says. He's standing there as if she hadn't embraced him.

What am I supposed to do about him. Stella has to squint because of the sun; she can't properly see Jason's face.

Do you want to hear my advice, Jason says, not waiting for an answer. You should stay out of it. You shouldn't react to it. I've read about this; reacting signifies contact; that's what it's about; that's what these people want. It's sick.

I'll stay out of it, Stella says. I'd stay out of it in any case. Where did you read this.

On the Internet, Jason says. On the goddamn, miserable Internet, where else.

*

Stella stands on the corner of Forest Lane and waves until the car with Jason in it has turned onto Main Street. She feels close to tears, and she doesn't know where they're coming from. Only later does she ask herself how she's supposed to stay out of something that she herself didn't cause; how is she supposed to control something that someone else is controlling. Jason's cigarettes are lying next to his coffee mug on the table in the kitchen. He's forgotten his jacket. He made the bed, leaving the bedroom window open. He read a report about a refugee camp in the newspaper; maybe he read the sentence, *Space changes; the relationship to places and spaces changes in times of war* before he got up from the kitchen table to drive to work, to drive off.

Six

Ava doesn't cry at all. But that evening she insists that Stella tell her a story. Stella should tell her some story. Ava won't take no for an answer. For Stella telling such a story is like a free fall. The characters that Ava wants to hear about tumble around in Stella's head, can only be held on to with great effort, they soar up and float off like helium-filled balloons.

Couldn't I tell you a fairy tale, Stella says weakly.

No, Ava says, firm and unrelenting. Tell me the story about the little giraffe and the prince.

Stella tries. She tries; afraid to think that, years later, she might regret never having told Ava the story of the little giraffe and the prince. (Back then. One evening in May. You were four years old, and Jason wasn't there. In that house in the suburbs where we used to live; I think you can still remember it a little. You had a room upstairs under the roof, your night-light was a globe; you always wanted to see the Atlantic Ocean on it. Outside your window there was the garden and a wild meadow; once we watched a buzzard; the buzzard caught a field mouse and flew away with it; you cried so hard; do you still remember? Back then. When I refused to tell you a simple story.)

This regret always stays with Stella. It is like a defect, like a tiny but important flaw in the system. Sometimes Stella thinks that Jason also feels this regret, but he passed the whole thing along to Stella; she took over his regret; she carries it with her. Why does she think this? Regret makes things difficult; at the same time unique, special.

*

The little giraffe can't fall asleep. She's lying next to the little prince and tries to close her eyes.

Tries desperately to close her eyes, Ava says.

Tries desperately to close her eyes. The little prince puts his arms around the neck of the little giraffe and presses his face into her furry coat. The little giraffe's coat is warm. The moon is shining through the window. The little giraffe says, I'm hungry. I'd like a glass of milk. The little prince gets up. The hallways in the castle are dark and very cold. In the kitchen the fat cook is sitting by the warm stove doing a crossword puzzle. She says, It's a good thing that Your Grace has come just now. Your Grace probably knows what falls from the sky and has four letters. And Your Grace probably wants a glass of hot milk?

*

Ava is lying on Stella's arm, her head on Stella's stomach. Her black hair is soft; her entire body is soft. She's twisting the buttons on Stella's cardigan; she sighs. She loves simple sentences; Stella knows that Ava is happiest with a story in which nothing actually happens. A story without a point, maybe also without any excitement, a story that tells about the uneventfulness of all days, about everything staying the way it is.

What falls from the sky and has four letters?

Rain. Rain falls from the sky and has four letters.

Snow also falls from the sky. Can I wear my red rubber boots tomorrow? No matter what? Even if it doesn't rain?

Tomorrow you can wear your red rubber boots, no matter what, even if it doesn't rain.

We were going to call Papa.

We'll do it tomorrow. Sleep well, Ava. Go to sleep quickly.

Stella leaves the door ajar and the light on in the hall outside the three rooms. She stands in the living room next to the armchair by the window; turning on the floor lamp, she looks at her reflection in the picture window, and behind her own reflection, the night-time garden, the fence, the street lamp and the street; the images slide into each other, depending on how she looks at them. Stella turns the lamp off again. She sits down at the table in the kitchen and makes a list of the things she wants to remember – *light bulbs, coloured oak tag for Ava, ask Walter about medication allocation, letter to Clara, weekend shift schedule, apples and pears* – she feels there's something else she should write down, that there was something she forgot; she can't think what it could be, and finally she gives up. The radio is softly playing classical music, series of discreetly withdrawn notes. Stella sits at the table holding a pen; she thinks that sitting here doing nothing at the day's end must be a sign of old age. How did she go to bed before? Before Ava? In the years with Clara, in the years before the decisions for this or that life or a completely different one were made. It seems to Stella that they used to go to bed while talking. Went to sleep still talking, got up again, talking. Went to bed drinking, smoking. Indignant or shaken – by what, actually? – or drunk. Used to fall asleep and wake up again precipitously. Everything was important. Everything was important.

The stillness at the kitchen table, the meaning of Ava's sleep, that her own encounters are limited to Jason, Paloma, Dermot, Walter and Esther, is odd. Suspect, as if it should mean something.

But I like being alone, Stella says aloud into the kitchen. I like being alone. Before this I didn't like being alone; now I just am.

She says, Mister Pfister presumably likes being alone too.

Mis-ter Pfis-ter.

What is Jason doing now, alone at the construction site, in the house without a roof, with doors of corrugated metal and floors of Alaska cedarwood. What is Jason doing? With whom actually would Jason like to talk?

*

Stella gets up from the table, runs water into the kettle, puts the kettle on the stove, and stands there until the water boils. She listens to the sound of the gas flame, the voice from the radio, the gradual bubbling of the water. She stands in the kitchen, waiting.

Seven

Rain.

Ava puts on her rubber boots, rain coat and rain hat, and, having done that, she looks long and seriously at herself in the mirror.

Stella pulls on her rain cape.

She goes to get the newspaper from the delivery man at the garden gate before he can drop it into the mailbox. Then she takes Ava to kindergarten on her bicycle and picks up Walter's keys from the office, arriving too late to have coffee with Paloma; she probably came too late intentionally. At Walter's house the porch door is wide open and the dampness hangs like a mist in the room, like fog. Walter's canaries are squeezed close together on the perch in their cage. Walter, lying on his side in bed, is pretending to be asleep, as if he had arranged it with Esther. Stella gently touches his shoulder. Would you like to get up, Walter?

Walter would not like to get up. Stella knows that she ought to force him to get up, but she feels much too weak herself. Walter is in his mid-fifties; he has multiple sclerosis. He was an architect, unmarried, childless; he likes to mention that he was an attractive man before the illness confined him to bed. Stella does not know him as an attractive man. She knows him as a patient, in need of help, dependent on her, ill. She knows his spit, his digestion, the smell of his urine. There are models of his work in the room: bridges and halls. Walter built mainly bridges and halls. Stella can't imagine his attractiveness, but she is touched by the delicacy and precision of the models, the accuracy and concentration that Walter was once apparently capable of. Whenever he wants to drink something nowadays, she has to put the straw to his mouth, to hold it in his mouth. On the wall around Walter's bed are posted pages of a newspaper series in which people talk about their dreams, having allowed themselves to be photographed for the series with closed eyes. Walter is crazy about this series, about the photos of the women, less about the description of their dreams, more about their faces, about their as-if-asleep faces. He keeps pretending that he's forgotten Stella's name and can't remember his mother any more, but he knows exactly when Wednesday comes around, the day the newspaper series appears. Today is Wednesday; Stella opens the newspaper in Walter's kitchen. A twenty-year-old blonde girl with an unfriendly narrow face and a dream that Stella doesn't feel like reading.

Will Walter want to put this girl up over his bed? Stella

assumes so. She isn't sure exactly what it is about these women's faces that is important for Walter – the closed eyes? They're to be near him but not supposed to see him in his helplessness? The desire to look at someone's face when you wake up. The desire as you wake up to see the sleeping face of the person you love. Stella feels she would go crazy if she were to think too long about Walter. Some of the carers consider Walter's gallery to be psychopathic. Stella doesn't express an opinion on the subject.

She cleans the bathroom, the kitchen, the refrigerator and the kitchen cabinets. She cleans out the birdcage, puts fresh water into the little dishes, hangs a new branch of hawthorn on the cage bars; the birds are sitting close together silently and reproachfully watching Stella with their black eyes. Carefully she hooks the little cage door shut and goes shopping.

She talks on the phone to Paloma and writes down Walter's doctors' appointments for the coming week. She mixes quark, plums and linseed; when she sits down next to Walter's bed, he doesn't even want to turn around to her, but he says he would be happy if they were to go to another concert soon. Stella sometimes does that. She goes out with Walter, to the movies, to a concert, to the theatre, and they can each put up with it for about half or three-quarters of an hour; then Walter says he wants to go home; he says it not just once; he says it a hundred times, says it until they're back again with the wheel-chair in the entrance hall of the large house in which his life is now confined to one room. Every time Stella is in complete agreement with what he says. In spite of that she keeps going out with Walter. She has the feeling that the resistance each of them has to overcome makes them both stronger. For a while at least.

She says, I'll go to another concert with you soon. Please turn around to face me. Have something to eat.

She feeds Walter and wonders if, concealed in the way he takes the food off the spoon she holds out to him, there's a little of the way he used to take food from the spoon his mother fed him with as a child. In Ava's way of eating, in that tiny final swallow, she still recognises the baby, still recognises Ava's baby-like snatching for the spoon, for the sweet porridge.

Walter's ancient mother might say that she recognises her baby in Walter. What a sad thought.

Walter, would you like to go outside?

Walter doesn't answer and Stella disregards this; she gets him out of bed. Dresses him, lifting his arms and dangling legs; she pulls thick socks over his ice-cold feet, puts on his useless slippers; then she wraps a scarf around his neck and, covering the wheelchair with his rain cape, she pushes him out onto the porch. She makes some tea and sits down with him. They sit next to each other, looking out into the rain, watching as the rain turns the tropical wood of the porch floor darker and darker.

A cold May.

Walter nods.

Stella unfolds the newspaper and holding it out to him, points to the blonde girl; he squints sceptically, then he waves it aside. There's something missing in the blonde girl. Or something is too much. How would she tell Jason about this? How can one share such things, this and that, also the tenderness she is capable of when wiping Walter's mouth, wiping his mouth with a napkin and, if she hasn't got a napkin, then with the palm of her hand.

The linseed is used up, Stella writes with chalk on the slate on Walter's kitchen cabinet for the evening shift. *Next week the freezer compartment should be defrosted. Water delivery cancelled? Best regards.*

She puts Walter back to bed, arranges the pillow roll under his head, covers him, and tucks the blanket neatly around his feet. She closes the porch door and tilts it.

Do the birds have food? Water? Walter's pronunciation is slurred, as if he were drunk, as if he were telling a joke.

Of course, Stella says. Enough till the end of the year, Walter. See you tomorrow. Take care.

She locks the front door from the outside. Wonders if he can hear that. And what it might sound like to him.

*

A wind that smells of the sea is blowing through the streets outside. Stella turns around. Quite a few people. No one she might recognise or know.

*

She goes to pick Ava up from kindergarten. She pulls on Ava's rubber boots, buttons up her jacket, puts the rain hat on her head and gently ties it under Ava's round chin.

I want ice cream.

I definitely want to have a cat. Definitely.

I want to visit Stevie. I want to be with Stevie all the time.

I drew a picture for Papa. I drew a house without a roof, but the others just drew a roof on it; they just drew a roof on top of it.

They cycle home through the rain. The sand at the edge of

Forest Lane is wet; the trees are almost black with wetness. Stella pushes the bike into the garden, lets the gate fall shut behind her, lifts Ava out of the seat and sets her down. Ava stands there, tilts her head back, holds her face up to the rain.

Stella unlocks the mailbox. There's a card lying in the mailbox. One side of it is white, blank, on the other there is just one sentence; the writing blurred, hurried – *those were long days.*

*

Come, Stella says to Ava. Let's go inside the house.

Eight

Clara phones in the afternoon. Her voice on the telephone is hoarse and absent-minded, so familiar and close, as if Stella could touch her; it is a huge relief to hear Clara's voice.

Stella, Clara says. Before we talk about anything else. Your new admirer – what sort of guy is he? Can you tell me what sort of guy he is?

She says it casually and distractedly. She says it as if she were chewing gum. As if Stella would even consider getting to know Mister Pfister. As if that were really still a possibility – one man among many, and yet the only one, just as in the past, wouldn't it be possible? Clara asks this as if Jason didn't exist. As if Jason didn't yet exist or not any more.

Clara, Stella says firmly. He isn't my admirer. In any case, he certainly isn't the type who would court me in some wacky way or other. Do you understand what I'm saying?

Oddly enough Stella knows this. She knows that Mister Pfister's interest in her is nothing like the interest of those who ten years ago dropped letters and cards into her mailbox, scratched symbols into the doorsill, and who, pushing past Clara in the hall, would sit down at the kitchen table, a bottle of schnapps in one hand and in the other a hand-rolled cigarette: Is Stella home, your roommate, you know, the pale, blonde; oh, she isn't, well then I'll just wait for her here, don't let me bother you; I'll just sit down here; she's sure to come back soon, isn't she. Ten years ago it sounded different when someone knocked unexpectedly on the door; so it seems. Perhaps Stella could say that Mister Pfister is the Finale. The final summing up of all those who had stood outside her door during the years she spent with Clara in the city.

Stella says, Mister Pfister is a damned ghost.

She's sitting at the kitchen table, drinking water, having peeled herself a green apple and cut it into little boats as she does for Ava; she eats the apple deliberately. Piece by piece, like a form of defiance. Clara, a thousand kilometres away, is also sitting at her kitchen table. At the cluttered table in her watermill under a small square window, her children in kindergarten, Clara's husband at school, the table full of cups and brushes, paints and glasses, nuts, fruit and candlesticks. Clara's beloved clutter, her hopeless chaos. Clara is drinking tea. But not eating an apple with it, smoking instead; she puffs audibly, and she is sketching; Stella can hear the sound of the pencil drawing on paper.

She says, Mister Pfister is a retribution. He is a punishment.

Punishment for what, Clara says.

I don't know, Stella says darkly. I haven't found out yet, but I think I will soon, I'll know soon, I'll figure it out. Do you remember the man on the tram?

The memory of the man on the tram has come back to her at just that moment. How long ago was it, fifteen years? A stranger, and she had got off the tram with him, walked quite matter-of-factly along the entire street all the way to hers and Clara's house, wordlessly climbed up the stairs, and finally arrived in the luckily empty apartment and gone to bed without any further ado. In the bright middle of the day. In Clara's bed.

Not her own, but Clara's bed. As if the encounter weren't real, hadn't taken place or had happened to someone else; Stella as Stella wouldn't have dared to do anything. Only as Clara had she been up to it – hold out your hand, close your eyes – and this way, but just one single time.

She says, the man with whom I went to bed, without knowing him. Who I never saw again after that. I don't remember his name, could also be that he never even told me his name, nor I mine, probably. My name is Stella? I never said that. But I remember everything else in detail. I dropped all scruples.

Actually I'm reserved, shy, Stella thinks, surprised. Was I always like that? Does Jason want me to be reserved? But in any case it makes no difference as far as Mister Pfister's interest in her is concerned. Mister Pfister's interest is a completely different type, and maybe it's precisely this that makes it so humiliating.

She says, I don't know any more whether I locked the apartment door in case you'd come home. You didn't come home. I didn't have to tell you about it, but I did tell you. I asked you whether I should put fresh sheets on the bed; the man wasn't clean, in a way you wouldn't have liked. In contrast to me.

What did I say, Clara says; she sounds interested now.

You said, No need to.

Stella has to laugh about it; Clara laughs too. Knowingly, probably wistfully; it's so pointless.

So you do remember now, Stella says.

Yes, Clara says, I remember. And why are you telling me?

Because Mister Pfister is the exact opposite, Stella says; she straightens up and takes a deep breath. I'm probably telling you because he is the exact opposite. Well, in any case he comes by here every day. Every day. When Jason is here, he doesn't; since Jason left, he's coming again. Rings the bell, puts something in the letter box, doesn't even wait any more; he knows that I'm here, that I won't come out; he knows it very well.

Stella gets up, goes to the sunroom, opens the screen door and stands in the doorway. May sunshine on the lawn; the trees cast hard, precise shadows. The lilac is withered, the flower-clusters are brown. A biting wind blows around the corner of the house, and the clouds near the horizon move swiftly.

Mid-thirties? Maybe he's in his mid-thirties. Stella thinks it would be better not to talk any more about Mister Pfister, it's not doing her any good, but she can't back off. She says, Actually he looks pretty good. Youthful, open, you know what I mean, but it's as if … damaged, you know. He looks quite normal, just like the rest of us, but something else comes through from underneath, exhaustion, neglect. Misery. Are you listening?

Yes, Clara says, surprised. I'm listening to you.

Stella listens for sounds. Then she says, He's absolutely alone. He acts as if he had all the time in the world. Endless amounts of time. By now I've seen him scores of times walking away from our house down the street, and he doesn't look like a man going to work. He wears unremarkable clothes, a dark jacket, light-coloured jeans; he never has a briefcase, never a book or a newspaper or a mobile. But always a packet of tobacco, always cigarette papers, always a lighter.

She thinks about it. Then she says, with hostility in her voice, He smokes constantly.

She says, I'm certain his fingers are yellow from the nicotine. Index finger and middle finger; Stella can feel that she's talking herself into a fury that might seem suspicious to Clara; nevertheless she keeps talking. He lives on our street. Five or six houses away. Jason walked by it. I haven't. Maybe I ought to do that sometime? I think he considers himself somewhat superior; you can tell from his handwriting. In any case, his spelling is correct and he listens to classical music; he wrote that to me. I have the feeling he got stuck. He got stuck; one day or other in his life something just didn't keep going; he's caught in a time warp and thinks he can pull me into it with him – that's what it looks like.

Stella says, Do you follow me, and she listens to Clara's thoughtful silence on the other end of the line, Clara's thoughtful silence in her oh-so-distant life. But today, just as back then, Clara still prefers to sit in the kitchen and, Stella knows, she has her feet up on the chair and the telephone clamped between her head and shoulder because she has to hold the cigarette in her left hand and the pencil in her right.

Clara, I'm asking you whether you can follow me. What are you drawing?

I can follow you. I'm drawing spirals, of course, Clara says drily. I'm drawing a time warp.

And how should I visualise that, Stella says.

Well, like a black hole, Clara says. A spiral, a very delicate one; I drew a delicate spiral, more of a vortex. In the middle, a black hole. Undertow or a deep void. The deep void in which Mister Pfister got stuck, that's what I'm drawing, it's obvious.

Please cut it out and send it to me, Stella says. Write something comforting under it, maybe something botanical. As if the spiral were something beautiful, a plant.

I will, Clara says. Already doing so.

*

Back then – in the apartment in the city, in the three rooms of which Clara had the left one, Stella the right one, and the middle room had only a sofa, the telephone and always a bunch of flowers – Clara had cut a poem out of the newspaper and hung it up on the apartment door. And the poem had stayed there until they moved out. The last line, as far as Stella can remember, was, *Let everyone in, whoever may come*.

*

Do you remember the title of the poem you hung up on our door?

House Rules. The title of the poem was *House Rules*.

Stella says, that's right. *House Rules*. Now I remember. If you were here, it would still apply. I would have to let everybody in, and I would have let Mister Pfister come in too. Would have invited him into the kitchen and put a cold beer on the table for him.

But Clara isn't here, and without Clara the commandments of these *House Rules* are defunct. Mister Pfister seems to know this; perhaps it's precisely because of this that he began to take note of Stella, Stella without Clara's protection and apparently without Jason's protection as well.

Do you think I should let him in? Open the door for him and speak to him?

No, Clara says slowly, and her voice sounds so earnest and profound that Stella suddenly becomes quiet. No, you should not let him in. Shouldn't open the door for him, or talk to him either. You should look out for yourself. Stella. Will you do that?

Nine

Now Mister Pfister comes by every day. He has figured out that Stella is trying hard not to be at home in the mornings, changing her shifts, starting them as early as possible, or being somewhere else; three times already she's sat in a café in the pedestrian zone, trying vainly to read a book, drinking tea with milk, eating a plain croissant, and feeling like a stranger in her own life.

Mister Pfister has caught on. That's Jason's expression – Mister Pfister has caught on, and so he just comes by a little earlier or a little later; even though he knows that Stella won't come to the door, it's important that she's there when he rings the bell. He knows when she is there; he knows almost always, and Stella can't think where he's actually observing her from. When Ava is there, he doesn't ring, but she feels it's only a matter of time, a matter of days before he'll ring when Ava is at home too. What comes to Stella's mind? A flood. The level rising. A deadline approaching, a time limit expiring.

Mister Pfister rings at the garden gate. He waits a precisely measured moment, drops something into the mailbox, goes on his way. He never turns around; he always passes the house and walks on. Stella no longer stands in the hall by the door. She stays wherever she is when he rings. Sometimes she's sitting in her room at her desk and sees him coming; he comes along the street from the left, and she leans back, closes her eyes, counting his steps. She whispers: Four, three, two, one more – now, and then the bell rings; if the window is pushed up, she can hear the clatter of the mailbox. She keeps her eyes closed, counts his steps to the street corner, keeps counting, and when she opens her eyes, he's already gone the length of Forest Lane and is out of sight.

Every day.

There's a letter in the mailbox. A card, an envelope, a scrap of paper, or a letter, and Stella takes a shoebox with her to the mailbox and drops the letter, the card, the envelope, the piece of paper into the shoebox, unread; she pushes the cover down on the shoebox as if there were something inside it that might offer resistance, and puts the shoebox on the floor in the shed under the workbench.

Tuesday, Wednesday, Thursday, Friday.

Friday is a warm day. The early morning sky, a transparent blue. Stella argues with Ava about whether or not shoes are necessary for the trip to kindergarten. At least she gets her to wear a jacket. In the child seat Ava triumphantly sticks her bare feet up in the air.

You have no idea what hot is. In kindergarten today we'll be allowed to go swimming. Are you going to buy strawberries? Can you buy ice cream? Can we turn on the lawn sprinkler soon? I love it when it's hot. I love when it's summer. Stevie loves it too when it's summer.

Stella listens to Ava's voice, Ava's self-absorbed questions, she can hear satisfaction in Ava's voice. Satisfaction in her clear observations, unambiguous feelings. I love summer. I love hot weather. Stevie loves summer too.

Do you love summer? Ava leans far to the left so as to be able to see Stella from the side; the bicycle wobbles. Ava puts her arms around Stella's stomach from behind.

Yes, I love summer too. Sit up straight, or we'll fall over. But I like winter better. I like it better when it's cold and it snows and is stormy.

Why?

Oh well, why.

The lawn at the kindergarten is shady and cool. The round table has been set for a second breakfast under the trees. Stella greets the kindergarten teachers from afar; she's afraid there might be questions about Ava, remarks that might alarm her. The shadows of the tree leaves dance over Ava's face, she looks so wide awake, she gives Stella a firm, untroubled child's kiss.

Tomorrow we're going to Papa.

Yes, tomorrow we're going to Papa.

*

Stella cycles home. She pushes the bicycle to the back of the house, unlocks the sunroom door with the key that's kept under the watering can, thinking that she should take the key inside the house, but then she puts it back under the watering can. She leaves the door open. Washes the dishes in the kitchen, makes tea, turns the washing machine on and the radio off, and sits down with the newspaper at the kitchen table.

Mister Pfister rings the bell at nine twenty-three.

Stella, her head propped in her hands, looks closely at a photo of some Chinese mine workers. Black faces, iridescent eyes. She reads the caption without understanding a single word. She turns one page back, then forward again. After a while she gets up from the table and goes into the living room, casually, just a woman looking out of the window, nothing more. The street is deserted. Nobody standing outside the garden gate. Nothing moving.

Stella closes the sunroom door, takes her jacket from the coat rack in the hall, and leaves the house. She doesn't look inside the mailbox. Pulling the garden gate shut behind her, she turns left and walks down the street.

*

A dog is lying in the sun outside the house next door. The front door is open; the student – Political science? Medicine? English literature? – who sometimes, either shyly or rudely, says hello over the fence, is nowhere to be seen. Her dainty vests and yellow dress hang on the rotary clothes dryer on the lawn; the grass hasn't been cut; the flowerbeds are neglected; sunflowers are already shooting up in several flowerpots. The picture window is dusty; in its right-hand corner, a skeleton, its bony hand held up in warning; candles in bottles on the windowsill. Stella looks at the display; she has the distinct feeling that it all has a meaning, a hidden message.

The house of the Asian family next to it is freshly painted; the garden, well cared for, the hedge trimmed and almost impossible to see through, a silver car in the driveway, the blinds down at all the windows.

An old woman one house farther on is clipping the branches of a rhododendron with huge garden shears; she greets Stella indulgently, and Stella greets her in return as she goes by, then she passes an empty, undeveloped lot. Stella vaguely remembers a house burning, an accident. Fallow land, yarrow and lupines, dried-out soil, no birds, finches, wrens in the grass. Next, a house with a glittering pool on the lawn, another one with an awning extending over the picture window and the terrace in front, an ironwork table, four chairs set around it as if for an important meeting. And then a house with a man sitting out front on a folding chair, setting the spokes in a wheel; on the stairs leading up to the front door a portable radio is playing; a mirrored sphere hanging in the branches of a sumac between the two properties throws spectrally coloured points of light on the house and the lawn. The man raises a hand. Stella has seen him before – where was it, in the city, at the shopping centre, at the kindergarten? She saw him at the kindergarten, a bicycle mechanic; he was fixing the children's bicycles. A boat lying under a tarpaulin, old bicycles leaning against each other in the rear part of the garden. Something makes Stella pause, and the man gives the wheel a push and sits up. *Carlyle was in a spot, he'd been in a spot all summer, since early June, when his wife had left him*, a voice on the portable radio is singing. Stella can hear each and every word clearly; she can see everything in detail, heightened and exaggerated; possibly it's because her heart is beating rather fast that she feels as if she were afraid. But afraid isn't the right word. She sees the wheel slowing down and coming to a stop, sees the man lean back in his chair; the chair is standing on sand, the garden path isn't paved; the sand is dazzling, summery. The next house is Mister Pfister's house. Number 8, and Stella looks away and walks on before she can change her mind. She can still hear the voice on the radio. A man softly and suggestively whistling to himself. Then she's there.

*

Mister Pfister's house is white. A grape vine grows skyward next to the front door. The grass is bleached. No flowerbeds, no garden chairs, no clay pots, no table, no umbrella. Nothing.

His house sits there, silent and still, in the midday sun. Orphaned. Stella has to squint, then sees that the picture window has been draped on the inside with some dark material, the small window next to the door also seems to be blocked with something, and the panes of glass in the door are black.

Grass grows in the cracks between the steps. For some intangible reason it's as if the front door hadn't been opened in a long time, as if Mister Pfister went in and out through the back door or through the chimney. Stella stands by the garden gate. She feels dizzy and hot. She has her hands around the rusty braces of the fence, looking at it all; there's something gratifying about being able to look at it all. It's like getting satisfaction, how do you say, it is like an appropriation. Stella feels that she oughtn't to be doing this – she shouldn't even be here. She is doing the opposite of what Jason advised her to do; she is reacting even though Mister Pfister doesn't even know anything about her reaction. But she can't help it. She cannot resist. She looks at his house the way he looks at hers; her eyes follow his route without holding back, without any affection. She also knows that the way he looks at her house, at her home, lacks all affection. Somehow or other, she knows it.

Mister Pfister's mailbox is old and dirty. Stella turns around; there's no one in sight. She lifts the cover. Feels the perspiration running down her spine. The mailbox is brimful. Advertisements, direct mail, window envelopes. Stella takes out a letter, an official letter from a bank, and stuffs it back into the mailbox. So, even if she were to write to Mister Pfister, her reply would never reach him. Mister Pfister, it seems, doesn't read his mail; nor does he seem to want to receive any more, and Stella has a sudden inkling about the inside of his house: mountains of paper, piles of newspapers, garbage bags, the kitchen half dark, the table full of things, things that from Mister Pfister's point of view might change their form any minute, their shape, their purpose and their identity. A bizarre, glowing, toxic wave of chaos sloshes from the house over the doorsill out into the garden, flowing towards Stella, and Stella lets the cover of the mailbox drop and backs away.

*

She wipes her hands on her trousers.

Then she goes home.

Past the man on the folding chair, past the terrace with the wrought-iron table that has now been set and at which a child and three grown-ups are sitting; only the child looks up. Past the fallow land over which downy poplar pollen is already flying, past the house with the rhododendron, past the silent house of the Asian family, past the house next to hers, in front of which the dog is just getting up, yawning and stretching his rear legs;

she walks towards her own garden gate, following the same route Mister Pfister takes daily, walking in his energy field. At what moment did he decide that his life should have something to do with hers. How long has he been walking down this quiet street past all these houses and finally past Stella's and Jason's house, thinking there was something that he could discuss only with Stella and with no one else. Since when has he known when Stella is at home and Jason isn't. How long did he think about ringing at her gate before he actually did ring.

Days?

Weeks or months.

Maybe Mister Pfister has been thinking about Stella for months already. Stella hadn't even known that he existed. There must have been a moment – in the street on her bicycle with Ava, at the shopping centre standing in the queue at the cash register, in the park with Walter in a wheelchair, on the bench by the fountain, in the pedestrian mall walking arm in arm with Jason, or someplace entirely different. Stella alone at the other end of the world – where he saw her, where he noticed her. There must have been a beginning. When was that.

Ten

Dermot and Julia's kitchen is warm. Julia is sleeping. She had something to eat, a soft-boiled egg and half a slice of bread; she drank some water and took her midday medications, primarily painkillers. She's lying on her side on the chaise longue in the living room, the blanket between her knees. Stella can see her through the open door. Lying there like that, she looks like a young woman, like the woman she once was, a tall, slender woman with short hair, eyes spaced far apart, arms that were too long, and terribly attractive; it's what Dermot says; Julia was so terribly attractive as a young girl, it was almost unbearable. The chaise longue is brown. The blanket is green-and-magenta-striped. Julia is wearing a grey dress. She doesn't care at all what Stella dresses her in; Dermot puts the things in which Stella is supposed to dress Julia on a chair, and Stella slips the dress over her head while holding Julia's head which is as heavy as a baby's. Stella believes that Dermot chooses these things carefully. Dresses he thinks are beautiful. Dresses that Julia once thought were beautiful. Dresses that aren't simply reduced to serving a purpose, and in which she wouldn't be humiliated. Today's dress has a delicate button tape on the collar, the buttons are round and made of worn mother-of-pearl. The hem is embroidered. Julia, sleeping on the chaise longue, enveloped in the darkening colours of the stormy afternoon doesn't look like a sick woman, one who is dying, but like a picture. Stella looks at her, blinks. She is tired; lately she's been tired all the time.

Dermot pours Stella a glass of water and sets it down in front of her. Outside, a worker apologetically pulls a plastic tarpaulin over the kitchen window; he looks into the kitchen as if into an aquarium, surprised but at the same time interested. The house, which doesn't belong to Dermot and Julia, is old, and it's going to be renovated and then sold. They have been granted a period of time still, but they will have to move out. By that time, Dermot may perhaps already be by himself. He'll have to pack up the things of their life together by himself – books, music, above all the books and the music, but also a lot of pictures, drawings, framed photos, boxes of papers, and cabinets full of correspondence in file folders, not to mention the dishes in the kitchen, the tables and chairs, shelves and lamps, armchairs and sofas, the harmonium and the brown chaise longue. In the cellar there's still a rocking chair, Julia's ice skates in a leather bag. Dermot doesn't talk about these things. Stella watches him. He doesn't act as if everything were finite. He has been married to Julia for sixty years. No children. No relatives. When Julia dies, and Stella thinks this will happen fairly soon, Dermot will be alone. The situation is so obvious that it seems simple. Dermot might perhaps say he was prepared for it. Maybe he would say that – I'm prepared for it.

He is short and a little hunchbacked. His head is too large. His manner is so gentle and self-effacing that Stella, even though she has spent only a short time with him, has felt for quite a while that she could be a better human being from now on. A more pleasant, kinder human being, grateful. Dermot's kindness is transmitted to her, is also transmitted to other people with whom they come in contact – Paloma, the irritable nurses in the hospital, the exhausted Indian doctor, the ill-humoured ambulance driver, the woman who cuts Julia's still-dark and very soft hair, the construction workers who are erecting the scaffolding around the house, ripping up the roof, spreading tarpaulin, scraping plaster, and who can't wait to do it, regretfully, can't delay no matter what – all of them take a step back, collect and calm themselves, try to smile, for once try to do things differently. That's Dermot. Stella can't say how Julia reacts to Dermot. Julia was already too far gone; she was already too far gone when Stella came to their house. It's possible that Dermot's kindness, his pleasantness is tied to Julia's illness. That can't be ruled out. But Stella also sees this kindness in the photos standing on the shelves, forty-year-old poses. Dermot and Julia at the seashore, Julia is walking out of the picture with a terribly attractive smile, Dermot is sitting on a round boulder, his face turned to the photographer, his shoulders hunched, and his hands between his knees. The horizon is blurred and almost unrecognisable. A pier jutting into the water lost in the indefinite. Where was that taken?

Ah well, where was that, where had that been. Dermot says he has forgotten, and he laughs about it. In any case, it was in March? Maybe it was March.

The kitchen is now in twilight. The construction workers are scraping plaster as if they were tearing the house apart. The windowpanes quiver. Stella looks at the clock. She can stay another half hour. She'll stay another half hour. Dermot sits down with her. He arranges Julia's pill boxes on the table, presses sky-blue, white and red pills out of their foil wrappings and sorts them into the dispenser; he counts softly under his breath, leafs through the prescriptions, says, Multimorbidity. Do you find this word as absurd as I do? He says, Drink your glass of water before you leave. Stella knows that formerly, when Julia wasn't yet sick, he was always the first to get up in the morning, to bring her a glass of water in bed. Julia, at dawn, in the early morning light, leaning back in bed, the window open and, outside, the beginning of an ordinary day. That was taken for granted. Dermot is still the first one to get up. Julia continues to lie in bed; were she to drink a glass of water, she'd have to throw up. That also is taken for granted.

I will, Stella says.

She watches him for a while, then plucks up her courage. She says, Do you know what it's called when you fall in love like a flash? When love hits you like a lightning bolt, like an accident. I know that there's a word for it, but I can't think of it.

She turns her glass on the table, trying to look distracted. She knows Dermot likes her. They each feel devoted to but also wary of the other, a shy trust.

Dermot closes the pill dispenser. He pulls his sweater sleeves down over his wrists – he always wears the same black sweaters, the wool at the wrists is always unravelled and full of holes – and looks at Stella, maybe slightly bemused but also surprised, forthright.

Did that happen to you? He says it as if he would be glad if it had happened to Stella.

No, Stella says, it didn't happen to me. Maybe what happened to me with Jason was love at first sight, that's what I had with Jason. But that's not what I mean. I mean the opposite of that – the same feeling but with something destructive about it, something not good.

Dermot mulls it over.

Then he says, You mean coup de foudre. A Love Thunderstorm, that's what you mean. The destruction comes from the lightning. From the force, the power of the lightning.

He smiles at that as if it were something quite wonderful. Wait. Wait a moment.

He gets up and goes from the kitchen into the living room, past the chaise longue, not touching Julia, he could straighten her blanket or touch her shoulder, but he doesn't, and she doesn't move; remains as this picture in soft colours, a woman sleeping. Stella watches as Dermot opens the drawers of his desk, rummaging around in a box for a while, putting it aside with a sigh, then going from there to the shelf and pulling out books. He blows the dust from their spines, opens them and closes them again, and finally comes back to the kitchen with a postcard. He pushes the pill boxes aside and puts the card down on the table in front of Stella.

A picture, an abstract painting, a figure the way Ava still draws them – a round head with braids, ears that stick out, and saucer-like eyes, from which arms and legs grow like feelers.

The expression of the figure is sorrowful; she looks as if she had been bashed to pieces, destroyed and demolished, irreparably; nothing here can be healed. A bolt of yellow lightning flashes through the body. Arrows directed down from above, and in the background another figure, male and shadowy, one body and two heads.

Something like this?

Yes, something like that, Stella says haltingly. But maybe more the other way around. Is the girl with the braids experiencing the coup de foudre, the lightning? Or that shadowy figure in the background. The male figure. She points with her index finger to the two heads, to the head on the right.

You can see it either way, Dermot says. I don't know. In any case, you can't defend yourself against being loved.

Mister Pfister's look at me must have been like this, Stella thinks. And now I'm like the girl in the picture; I'm falling.

Are you all right, Dermot says.

Oh yes, I'm all right, Stella says. I'm all right. I'm up against someone to whom this happened; you understand, this happened to him in connection with me.

She feels she is blushing, it embarrasses her to say this. I have to deal with it. I just have to learn how to deal with it.

Probably not easy, Dermot says. Oh my, this probably isn't easy.

That's all he says. And there is nothing more to say, Stella thinks. They sit together in silence and listen to the pounding of the construction workers, pounding on wood, stone and concrete, repeated, like a vague request to be admitted, a notification of some difficult task, and even if it's just one single word.

Julia turns over on the chaise longue. Stella listens, but Julia doesn't call her.

I think you always have to try to come to some arrangement, Dermot says. He says it as if he had thought about it for a while already. To find a midpoint between sympathy and indifference. Indifference is very important. I don't mean coldness, I mean something more like cool-headedness, composure. Maybe you shouldn't take it to heart? All this will pass, that much I can tell you.

Stella nods. Suddenly she has to think of Jason as clearly as if he had called out to her. As if he were falling from the roof at his construction site and calling to her. She has to think back to her first sight of Jason – serious and angry, on his part as well as on hers. Serious and angry; one of them shrank back from the other, and for the first time she realises that this is how it was.

She would like to ask Dermot whether he remembers his first glimpse of Julia. A glimpse that goes back more than sixty years. But she doesn't have the nerve. She repeats his last sentence like a question, and she can tell from the expression on Dermot's face as he turns around, that this isn't the truth either. Not something that one could know with finality, once and for all. Not something for always.

*

That evening she is sitting at the kitchen table with Ava; they're eating together. White bread and green tomatoes. Ava tears the bread up methodically and completely, drinks her juice in thirsty swallows; in kindergarten she drew a cat with long whiskers and big eyes. The cat now hangs on the wall above the chest. Stella can see the wild meadow through the window, storm clouds over the wild meadow. It's not yet late; in spite of that, almost dark. Ava was allowed to light the candle on the table.

She says, The cat looks stupid.

She says, I would always like to sit next to Stevie in the morning circle. Always. I never want to sit anywhere else in the morning circle. Do you know what Stevie wants to be?

No.

A fireman. Ava leans across the table and whispers. He wants to be a fireman or a spy.

Aha, Stella says. Something about Stevie seems odd to her, and Ava senses it; she frowns angrily and changes the subject. I'd like to take a bath. And I don't know at all what I should wish for my birthday. What should I wish for my birthday? I want to have a garden party. Go to the circus. Do you think the cat looks stupid? I like it when we sit in the dark. Oh, I wish it would rain soon.

Ava turns to the window.

Stella says, I think the cat looks clever. Like a magician.

The doorbell rings. Hard, long and decisively.

Ava says, That's Papa. Is that Papa?

She says it without turning around, and for one unreal moment Stella thinks that Ava knew the bell would ring. That she turned to the window so that Stella couldn't see her face.

Stella says, No that isn't Papa. Papa has a key. He never rings the bell.

Ava waits, listening. Then she does turn around to Stella and puts her hands on the table, looking at Stella, subdued; she sits there very quietly.

Why don't you open the door.

Because we don't want any visitors. We don't want any visitors, do we. It's late, we're just having supper, you have to go to bed in a little while, you still want to take a bath, we have to pack your little bag because tomorrow we're going to see Papa; we have no use for visitors now.

But who's ringing, Ava says. Who's ringing? She looks so alert, so wise; her eyes are shiny, round and strange.

Somebody or other, Stella says testily. Somebody or other, somebody we don't know and don't want to get to know. I don't ever want you to open the front door without me, not the house door and not the garden gate either; do you hear what I'm telling you? Do you understand me?

But why don't we want to get to know anybody, Ava says. She simply ignores Stella's question. Why not? Maybe it is better if you let him in and we can get to know him then.

Ava, Stella says.

She tries to imagine it. Simply to imagine it. Mister Pfister in the kitchen. In this kitchen next to Ava, sitting at the table. It's of course impossible.

She says, That's not possible; it's impossible; you have to accept this even if you don't understand. We have to wait and see. See how it will go on from here.

But I *do* understand, Ava says. I understand it exactly. And the cat *does* look stupid, I drew an ugly cat. I know that, and you know it too.

*

Mister Pfister doesn't ring again.

*

He rings the bell that night at two a.m., and Stella is instantly awake. She gets up and goes from the bedroom to the little room. She is awake because she has been waiting.

The street is dark. The storm has moved on; the street lamps are already out. In spite of that Stella can see Mister Pfister. This time he's walking in the other direction, home, and she can hear his measured, imperturbable steps in the night-time silence. For a long while still. She thinks she can almost hear Mister Pfister's garden gate slamming shut behind him. Where's he coming from at this hour.

Eleven

The week after Stella and Ava return from Jason's construction site the weather turns hot and summery. Twenty-eight, thirty, thirty-two degrees. Stella's alarm clock rings at five thirty. She turns it off and stays in bed, lying on her back, awake in her empty-without-Jason bed, feeling the morning coolness like a touch, precisely because it is so brief. At six o'clock in the morning the grass in the garden is damp and cold. A thrush perches in the hedge. The morning sun casts Ava's sandpit in shade so deep you could grasp it with your hands; at the edge of the meadow the first poppies are beginning to bloom. The sound of cars slowly rolling by the house, people on their way into the still-uncertain day.

*

Ava sleeps under a sheet; in the morning she lies there without the sheet, her arms stretched out in abandon, hair sweaty. The warm air enters the house like a guest. Stella breakfasts in the garden with Ava. She drinks tea, watching Ava engrossed in eating her porridge with berries, swinging her legs, then pressing her feet into the grass. All I need to wear is a dress, Ava says, serious. Just one single dress, nothing else.

At the kindergarten Stevie runs towards Ava, an expression of worried joy on his face; at any rate that's what it seems like to Stella. He is thin, has a fox fur hat on his head in spite of the heat, and doesn't give Stella even a glance. She holds Ava tight and says, Till later, Ava, till then. But Ava pulls away, has already turned away.

*

And where were you, Esther says. Where were you the entire weekend. You're certainly not the brightest but really, the other girls from your awful nursing service are even more stupid; they're all atrociously stupid.

Stella doesn't answer Esther when she's in this frame of mind, doesn't talk to her at all. She opens the windows and closes them again; lowers the Chinese rice-paper blinds, puts fresh sheets on the bed, and changes the flowers in the vases; she washes strawberries, cuts them up and sugars them.

I won't eat that, Esther says. I don't eat anything any more; I don't eat any of that stuff. Esther is sitting in her wicker chair, a wrinkled queen in sand-coloured underwear; she looks like an old, stubborn child. Her hair stands on end, her face glows. Stella lifts her into the wheelchair; for one moment they stand in a tight embrace in the middle of the room, Esther in Stella's arms, an invitation to the dance. Stella feels Esther's breath on her collarbone, feels Esther's fragility. She pushes Esther into the bathroom, lifts her onto the edge of the bathtub, puts Esther's feet into the tub and turns on the cold water; she washes Esther; then she sits on the toilet bowl and watches as Esther, eyes closed, lets the water run over the insides of her wrists, her arms, her knees. As if she were at a spring.

All right now, Esther says. Where were you. How was it. It's easy to see that you have some sort of problem. Tell me about it.

Stella has to laugh at this. She believes that Esther has cheated her way all through life with this faked interest in others whom she doesn't really want to know anything about, not about Stella and not about anyone else either. She *is* interested, but not in the details, more in the general, the overall picture. In world politics. The outcome of wars. War, in and of itself.

I was away in the country, Stella says. With my husband and my child. We went swimming. Everything's OK. I'll give you five more minutes here; then we have to go back to your room. You're going to eat the strawberries; I'll force you to.

Oh, what the hell. Go on, be like that, Esther says dully. Your husband and your child. I also had a husband and several children, and they're all gone. Up and away. Life is horrible; have you already discovered that?

She pushes Stella's hands away. Washes her face and neck by herself, still sitting on the edge of the tub, naked, an archetype.

*

During the lunch hour Stella cycles over to Paloma's office. Paloma has turned the cooling fan on the windowsill to the highest setting; a vigorous, artificial breeze blows through the room. In addition, Paloma is also using a paper fan to fan herself; she's barefoot, her tanned skin is shiny. She points to the chair in front of her desk; Stella obediently sits down. Paloma looks at Stella quizzically, then she folds up her fan and says, Well Jason isn't here, as if there were some connection between Stella's presence and Jason's absence. This isn't entirely mistaken. But it isn't correct either.

No, Jason has left again.

For how long this time, Paloma says, not waiting for an answer. She says, Let's go outside and put our feet in the fountain. Let's watch the sparrows.

She locks the office door, and Stella follows her through the stuffy foyer and out to the park. Dazzling light. Paloma is still barefoot and Stella takes off her shoes when they reach the fountain and sits down on the rim next to Paloma; she puts her feet into the water, supporting herself with her hands on the hot stone. No wind; the trees along the avenue stand motionless. Stella thinks she hears the kindergarten children's voices at the far end of the park. She's afraid Ava might come by, hand in hand with Stevie, in a column lined up two by two for a walk. She thinks again that everything in her life is too close together. Work, house, kindergarten. She longs for distances, distances to be covered; only Jason, Stella thinks, is always far away, too far away for me to reach him.

The sparrows bathe in the fountain, at a safe distance. Paloma pushes up her dress, submerges her wrists in the water; Stella can see little gold particles glittering in the bends of her elbows. She thinks of Esther on the edge of her bathtub, of Esther's dry skin, her sly look. Esther would have had something to say about the little gold particles.

I'm going on a trip this year, Paloma says. I'm staying at the summer house for a week; then I'll close it and go to visit my mother, driving on from there by car simply straight ahead until I arrive somewhere. Wherever that is. That's my plan.

They both shade their eyes against the sunlight and look down the park path as if something were coming towards them. The foliage is now dense and peacocks are calling from their hiding places. Stella imagines Paloma's mother, an old woman on a balcony in a development where, fifty years ago, there were many children and where today the clothes lines neatly stretched between wooden posts are empty. Perhaps Paloma's mother lives like that. Perhaps she lives completely differently.

Where do you sleep when you visit your mother.

I sleep on the sofa, Paloma says. I sleep on the sofa and wake up at night because the television set crackles. The housing of the TV crackles. Do you know that sound? Unpleasant. It's unpleasant.

She shakes her head, stands up and climbs out of the fountain; her footprints evaporate quickly from the stones.

I have to get back to work. The phone is ringing; I can hear it even out here, probably only imagining it. But the old people go haywire in this heat and die like flies. Like flies. Come inside with me. Stay with me a while until you have to go to Julia.

Maybe Paloma wishes Stella would talk. But Stella doesn't know what she should say. How she should explain her passivity, her waiting. What is she waiting for.

*

The tarpaulin outside the windows of Julia and Dermot's house seem to shade it from the heat, and the atmosphere in all the rooms is diffused. Stella washes Julia, dresses her, and takes her to the kitchen. Dermot goes shopping, to the library, for a walk; Stella doesn't know what he does when he leaves the house, when he frees himself for an hour from the togetherness with Julia. When he comes back, he has also brought strawberries. Julia is sitting on the bench in the kitchen leaning back against the wall, her head turned to one side, facing the blue light outside the window. In her lap is a silver spoon; Julia keeps putting her thumb into its bowl, feeling it. Dermot watches her. Then he says, I brought strawberries; naturally she says nothing in reply. Stella washes the strawberries; Dermot hands her a plate and then puts the plate with the strawberries on the table, in the exact centre.

Please sit down for another moment.

Stella sits down next to Julia. She wishes Dermot would ask her something, and he does, pleasantly. He clears his throat. Then he says, Did you get anywhere with your coup de foudre?

No, Stella says. She can't help smiling, as if she were lying. No, I didn't. We spent the weekend at the lake at Jason's construction site. In the house he is just building.

Dermot looks at her expectantly. Stella shrugs. What is there to tell? The house is on the shore, the framing shows where the walls will be; the windows haven't been set in yet; a house like an idea, a vision of a distant future. The opposite of Dermot and Julia's house, as well as the opposite of Stella and Jason's house. Views of the water, of the forest.

She says, It was the first warm weekend this year. We slept overnight in sleeping bags on the roof. Ate doughnuts, drank tea from a thermos; everything very makeshift; Ava liked it. Ava went swimming in the ice-cold lake.

Jays in the tops of the tall pines; warnings of something. Ava and Jason had vanished into the woods. Stella was sitting on an overturned paint pail in the middle of a room as large as a dance hall and thinking that she had lost one temporary arrangement after another in her life. Had thought about it with bitterness. But later Jason had laughed about it. He'd said, Changes will come again soon enough, Stella. Just wait. What is a temporary arrangement? Ava's question, and Stella had said, Papa and I are talking about two different things. Ava's hands, cupped together like a bowl, and in the bowl a stag beetle, iridescent and green. When they said goodbye, Stella had cried. Stella, not Ava.

She says, We had a quiet time. I felt detached. I'll have to see.

Julia doesn't turn to Stella. She is looking towards the window as if she were sitting in the kitchen by herself; the spoon in her lap turning like the needle on a compass. It doesn't matter to Stella. Still, it would be a gift if Julia would say something, unexpectedly, something simple and absolutely right.

The night under the open sky was beautiful, Stella says. The night under the open sky was actually the most beautiful part.

*

In the garden that evening at home Stella gets the lawn sprinkler out of the shed for Ava and turns it on. Ava squeezes her eyes shut, trembling in expectation before the jet of water pivots and falls on her; she stands under the lawn sprinkler, arms close to her body, hands balled into fists. Stella collapses the garden umbrella, sets the table. Two plates, two glasses. Too little. Voices from the other gardens, the slamming of screen doors, the chinking of ice cubes. The telephone rings, and Ava, soaking wet, runs into the house. It's Jason.

Is everything all right? How are you?

It's hot, Stella says. You're not here. We're all right.

*

And now Mister Pfister puts something into the mailbox every day.

A letter in a red envelope, sturdy, heavy paper, like an invitation to a children's birthday party, dropped in at three o'clock at night.

A letter in a yellow envelope with nothing on it but Stella's name.

An awful piece of graph paper covered with tiny letters from the first to the last square, an ants' scrawl with whorls and circles twining through them, all doodled with a ballpoint pen.

On Tuesday morning he puts a slip of paper into the mailbox with the word *Wednesday* on it.

He puts a Dictaphone into the mailbox. A USB flash drive. A self-burned CD in a sleeve sealed with gaffer tape. A small, transparent bag with some indefinable things inside – pips?

He puts a piece of cardboard into the mailbox; a symbol has been drawn on the piece of cardboard that perplexes Stella because it resembles the symbols somebody or other once scratched into the doorsill of Stella and Clara's apartment in the city ten years ago; three intertwined circular arcs, the symbol for an infinite connection; what does this symbol signify for Mister Pfister?

Mister Pfister puts a roll of twine into the mailbox. A burned-down match, a cigarette lighter and a dirty lollipop on a gnawed stick.

For one entire day he puts nothing into the mailbox, a nothing full of insinuations, a pulsating caesura.

Then he puts a sheet of music paper into the mailbox with scribbles between the lines of the stave and the clef thoroughly scribbled over.

I haven't been listening to music for a long time, Stella thinks. Anyhow, not for a long time.

She waits for mail from Clara. For Clara's perspective on Mister Pfister's abyss, the spiral with the botanical name, for her energetic protection. But it seems that Clara thinks Stella can take care of herself.

*

On Friday there's a photo in the mailbox. Stella tries not to look at the photo, and fails. On her way to the shed, to the shoebox, she stops in the glaring sunshine, holding the photo in her hand, bends down to look at it, studies it, can't help herself.

Is that Mister Pfister?

No doubt about it, it is.

Mister Pfister next to his mother or next to his grandmother, in any case Mister Pfister next to an older woman in a living room; the living room is gloomy, a couch, a low table, and a puny Christmas tree, half of its branches draped with tinsel. Mister Pfister's facial expression is indescribable. The woman beside him sits with staring eyes and seems petrified as if she were facing a serious threat; the atmosphere of the room is totally depressing. The room isn't a room in Mister Pfister's house, Stella is sure of that; the window behind the couch isn't the kind used in the housing development. Possibly it's a window in an apartment house, maybe a window in a high-rise building. The photo is out of focus, blurry, bad. It is so bleak that it makes Stella feel sick, a sick feeling somewhere between fear and anger. What is this photo doing in her mailbox anyway and in her hand. Why should she have to concern herself with a photo like this, with a stranger's private horror? Stella stands outside the shed with the photo; turning around, she looks across the garden out to the deserted street. Noonday. No shade, no birdsong, not a soul. She'd like to tear the photo into little scraps, but she has to show it to Jason, she has to pass it on, definitely must hand it over; she feels an intense need to wash her hands. The shed is stuffy and dark. The shoebox under the workbench has a pronounced heft.

*

That evening Stella sits by Ava's bed until Ava falls asleep. Ava's breaths changing from sighs, questioning sounds, into a slow rhythm that Stella listens to for a long time. Breathing as if there were nothing to fear in this world. Ava's tight grip on Stella's hand relaxes; then she lets go, turns onto her side and straightens her legs. Stella pushes up the window, switches on the night-light in the globe, and leaves the room on tiptoe. In the kitchen the radio is humming, the tap dripping, the remnants of their supper still on the table. For a while Stella leans against the door to the already dim living room with her arms crossed, then she goes into the kitchen, back to the living room, into the hall, and finally into Jason's room; she sits down at Jason's desk and turns on the computer. Sits there and watches as the screen lights up; then she enters the word *stalking* into the search field, one letter at a time.

To stalk – to hound, chase, walk stiffly, strut
Obsessive and abnormally long pattern of menacing

by means of harassment directed towards a particular individual

A manner of behaviour in which one person repeatedly forces unwanted communication and contact on the other person; the behaviour must occur several times and be perceived as undesirable and invasive, and it may cause fear and anxiety

To be categorised as the victim of stalking, at least two separate behavioural patterns that violated the private sphere of a person must have been reported, and whereas these must have continued for at least eight weeks and must be causing fear

It's almost funny. What is she supposed to do with such phrases. Delusion of love, reflection, psychological intimidation. Person. Strutting person. Boundary. Recognition of a boundary. Violation of a boundary. Stella's fingertips feel numb. She'd like to have a cold beer. Smoke a cigarette. Open a book. Go to sleep.

Did Jason read the same thing she did?

I read about it, Stella can hear Jason's voice. She turns off the computer, leans back, and remains sitting in Jason's environment that has now suddenly become disquieting; his mail, his glasses, his pencils, 6B pencils sharpened with the blade of his cutter and equipped with a protective silver cover. Photos above his desk and on the wall, Stella in the morning, an old model Lada Niva car, Ava lying on her tummy, her little head raised, a drop of saliva on her chin, and a photo of a suburban town on a river taken on the only trip Stella and Jason took together, a trip before Ava was born. What does the choice of photos imply.

And what does it mean that Stella is looking at them, not Jason. What does Jason's absence signify.

Stella tilts her head and looks for a long time at the photo of the suburban town. Innumerable balconies above and next to one another; the meadows along the river's edge, muddy; the water, glittering. Jason had said, This is where I'd like to live with you. The day had been rainy, they had walked hand in hand; Stella was pregnant and hadn't known. They didn't move to the development by the river. They moved into another housing development, into this one, and at some point they'll move elsewhere. Mister Pfister will stay here. He is going to stay here; he won't move elsewhere; that's how it will be.

Mentally, Stella counts off the days. Twenty-five – not even half of the eight weeks have passed. She gets up from the desk. Then she leaves the room.

Twelve

Jason comes back along with the cold. Steady rain and gusty wind; he's standing in the hall, already thoroughly soaked from the short walk through the garden from the car, and pushing his bag and backpack into the house with his foot.

You're here, Ava says.

She goes on sitting at the kitchen table, drawing her picture: a house in the woods surrounded by giant butterflies; she draws an endlessly long butterfly antenna, and Jason takes hold of her and lifts her up. He says, You're just like a cat, you're only pretending you're not glad to see me, and Stella sees Ava's chin quivering with joy.

Jason has brought a perch he caught himself. He's brought a sceptre carved from birchwood for Ava and a lake pebble for Stella. He is tanned and looks unkempt, unshaved. You're so scratchy, Ava says, and for one selfish moment Stella wishes she could be all alone with Jason.

You got very tall, Jason says. You've grown like crazy, both of you.

Like crazy.

Ava stands with her back against the door frame in the kitchen, and Jason draws a new line above her little head, one metre and three centimetres. Ava has grown two centimetres since the last line, a line drawn in the winter, in long-ago January. She continues to stand in the door frame and looks at the new line, proud and doubting.

How long will you be staying, Stella says. When do you have to leave again; she turns away before Jason can answer her.

*

They eat the fish that evening. Daylight fades away; rain falls outside the kitchen window like a wall. The barrel at the corner of the house fills up and overflows, the rain drums onto the outside metal windowsills and against the windowpane. Jason takes a bath. Ava sits down near him. Stella dries the dishes. Listening to their voices. Jason's stories about perch, sunken boats, about trips, and about the summer, Ava's questions.

It was very hot here when you were gone. So hot. In kindergarten we all played only in the shade, nobody wanted to go into the sun.

You have to do what the chickens do when it gets so hot.

What do the chickens do?

A chicken just lies down flat on the ground. As flat as possible, with its wings spread out. It lies down in the dust with outspread wings.

Ava says nothing. Then she says, we're not allowed to do that. In kindergarten. I'm sure we're not allowed to lie down in the dust, and Stella hears Jason's absent-minded laughter. She clamps Ava's picture under the magnet on the refrigerator. She unpacks Jason's bag, putting the book he's pretending to read on the bottom step of the staircase – he'll take it up with him later; the book on the night table will be like a sign of his presence – and she finds her joy at that puzzling and complicated. She opens the front door and looks out into the now-whispering rain for a while. Jason's car is in the driveway, a sign of his presence to the outside world; it's all much too simple. Mister Pfister won't ring the bell tonight. Whenever that car is parked in front of the house he'll busy himself with something else, and he'll collect all the things that are intended for Stella and put them all together. He'll save them up for Stella.

*

On the third evening she fetches the box from the shed. The garden, overwhelmed by the rain, is a fertile, lush wilderness. Honeysuckle, broom in bloom. The feeling of actually wanting to do something else and not knowing what and instead fetching this box out of the dirty darkness under the workbench is like a symptom. Stella carries the box across the lawn into the house. She is about to put it on the kitchen table and then changes her mind after all; she puts it on the floor, in front of Jason's feet, leaves it to Jason to lift off the cover.

She says, Careful.

Jason says, Good heavens.

He sits there bent over the box. Takes things out and lets them drop back in again. The lighter, the roll of packing twine.

He opens the red envelope that Stella didn't open, takes out a piece of paper with dense writing on it, leans back and reads.

What does it say, Stella says.

Can you just wait a minute, Jason says. He says, Please.

Then he says, Nothing bad. It doesn't say anything bad. But something … sick, incomprehensible. Drivel, Jason says it as if the entire world were held together by drivel, as if drivel were a principle of life.

He says, Here, take it; it's all right; you can read it.

He holds the piece of paper out to Stella, a little too close. Stella pushes it away.

I don't want to read it.

She looks at Jason and suddenly wonders whether it might be possible to understand Mister Pfister after all. Impossible for Jason maybe, but possible for her? She understands Dermot; she understands Julia's final, decisive silence; she understands Esther's irritability and Walter's indistinct speech; after all, she understands quite a few things; maybe she should just find out more about Mister Pfister's way of thinking. About the hints, the chorus of voices that seem to vibrate from the box. Also for strategic reasons. To know what makes Mister Pfister tick, how he functions.

But she says, I don't want to read any of that. None of it. I only want to know that there's nothing in there about Ava. Nothing that might signal something, do you understand? A threat, an intrusion, something that would go beyond this here.

This here. Gesturing at the box.

There's nothing about Ava in this, Jason says. He's reading as he says it; he's reading the page with the ant-like writing, shaking his head as he reads; he says, Disgusting, there's something disgusting about it. It's probably good that you don't want to read it. There's nothing in here about Ava and nothing about you. Nothing really about you.

What would a sentence about me be, Stella wonders. A sentence about me that would mean something to you, and the impossibility of finding an answer to this question is clear and stark. She thinks, I'm actually a mythical figure for Jason. A mythical figure. There's nothing that he could say about me really, no description that could apply to me.

Stella gets up. Now Jason is holding the photo and looking at it with a critical expression. He says, My goodness. This is the last straw, isn't it.

He holds up the photo; shows it to Stella as if assuming that she hadn't seen it yet. He looks at Stella, he sees that she is pale, but she doesn't seem pale enough for him to reach out to her, to touch her.

He says, I'll go by there. Tomorrow. Tomorrow I'll go over there.

He says, You were there already, weren't you. Passed by his place, didn't you.

No, of course not, Stella says. I haven't gone by his place.

As far as she can remember, this is the first time she has ever lied to Jason.

Thirteen

Jason takes Ava to her kindergarten on Stella's bicycle. He comes back, spends an hour at his desk with the door closed, looking through his mail and telephoning. Then, taking a garden chair to the edge of the meadow, he sits down there with his back to the house.

He brushes his hand from the back of his neck over his head, a gesture Stella loves – not that she would ever have told him that. She assumes that if she told him he would no longer do it.

*

She's sitting at her desk upstairs in her room, writing a letter to Clara – *the entire garden smells like a greenhouse, and in the evening the rabbits venture out of the field; Jason is back; I live like a war bride; you know, don't you, what I feel like? What is your life like, and how far removed is that life from the life we imagined ten years ago, and does it even matter* – She can hear Jason downstairs in the kitchen; the refrigerator door opening and closing again; he moves the chairs closer to the table and puts the dishes into the dishwasher that Stella never uses, and turns it on; then he sweeps the sunroom. He takes the bottled water crates out and sets them next to the car; goes back into the hall, closes the front door behind him, stands in the hall doing nothing; maybe he's looking through the little window at the garden. He goes back through the living room into the kitchen and seems to stop and hesitate next to Stella's armchair with all the books around it; if he were observant, he'd be able to see that Stella hasn't sat in that armchair for the last two weeks, not really read anything in it for two weeks; the pile of books is completely neglected; how observant is Jason actually, and which book is Stella trying to read just now in spite of everything; *I'm trying to read a book by an author in which there actually are sentences like: A man in love walks through the world like an anarchist, carrying a time bomb.* There's nothing more to do in the kitchen. Jason clears his throat; there's a note of warning in it. Then at last he comes up the stairs, stops at Stella's door, and says, Am I bothering you.

No, Stella says.

She puts the pen down on the paper and turns to face him.

*

Jason is sitting on the guest bed, his back leaning against the wall, his legs crossed, a rare visitor. Stella stays at her desk; suddenly she finds it odd to see Jason in her room surrounded by things that belong to her: on the same bed – under the shelf attached to the wall on which there sat a porcelain cardinal bird next to a snow globe, a golden Buddha, and a row of pebbles from the Black Sea – the bed on which, day after day, she had fallen into restless sleep at noon in the apartment she shared with Clara ten years ago. Stella's bookshelf, Stella's desk, her pens and candles, to Jason some surely foolish-seeming incense sticks, the pearl necklaces around the chair leg, the bird feather on the wall, and the orange cloth clamped for the last two weeks into the window frame and tied around the window handle, an orange cloth with white peacocks on it. Stella suspects that at some point Jason made contact with all this, made contact with Stella's world. As if he'd been on an expedition, maybe it was arduous, painfully slow. Has he, leaning back on her bed, arms crossed over his chest, and eyes almost closed, arrived now? Would he like to stay, or would he like to travel onward, or go back again, or somewhere else. Stella sees Jason's – to her beautiful and unapproachable – face. She feels that she can't change anything in his movements, wherever they will lead, forward or back, and surprisingly, this is bearable.

I'll just walk over there, Jason says.

He sits up, rubs his eyes.

He looks at Stella, he looks past her; he says, Is that all right with you? I'd just walk over there again.

Yes, Stella says. She smiles in a way that feels strange even to herself. She'd like to say, I'm sorry, but she feels that this sentence can't encompass the extent of what it is that she's sorry about; actually she doesn't even know what exactly she's sorry about. Is it an imposition for Jason to go over there? To deal with Mister Pfister because she has to deal with him?

It would be better if he stayed here. Stayed with her.

Well, see you then, Jason says.

See you soon, Stella says.

*

She waits in the garden. On the chair where Jason had been sitting. Noontime is very quiet. It's getting hot. In one of the other gardens a lawn mower starts up, and far away a child calls. Butterflies startle up from the lawn, the sky is grey. Someone rides past the house on a bike. Stella yawns.

After a while Jason comes back. He says, He wasn't there. Or he didn't open the door; that could be it too, but I think he wasn't there. What a neglected hovel.

Jason looks around, looks at his own house as if he were comparing it. From the outside, the effect of a window with broken shells lying on its sill. Empty bottles by the terrace door, Ava's jacket hanging over a spade handle.

Stella says nothing.

Nor does she say, I knew he wouldn't be there. It was obvious that he wouldn't be there.

Mister Pfister will never be there when Jason goes over there. He isn't answerable to Jason; he'll never be at home, never open his door to Jason.

*

But she runs into him when she goes shopping the following day. Early in the evening, at the shopping centre, at the checkout in the supermarket. She went there by bicycle, intending to buy milk, eggs, alphabet noodles, butter, nothing else; she decides to take a shopping basket instead of a cart, is walking to the turnstile through which you go to get inside the shop, when she sees Mister Pfister standing at the last cash register.

Hard to believe that he goes shopping. Gets hungry, wants to buy himself something to eat. Says please and thank you, good day, goodbye.

It's the first time Stella has seen him outside. In everyday life, there he stands, waiting in the queue at the checkout counter next to a cigarette machine under a monitor on which a weather forecast alternates with advertisements for car-body paint shops; in the background, the labyrinth of grocery shelves, pyramids of water melons, references to products, and over it all, hellish music. He's got the things he wants to buy assembled in a cardboard box; he holds the box to his chest, moves one mechanical step forward in the queue, a man like all the others, Mister Pfister exists.

Stella stops, stands there almost devoutly. She thinks, astonished, I didn't consider it possible that he existed. But he exists. He does exist after all. Here he is, he is here.

She recognises him from his posture, his expression; she is certain, yet she is surprised at how young he is, how good-looking and how tired. He's wearing a black hoodie sweater. No jacket any more, in spite of the early evening, early summer cold. She can't see what's inside his cardboard box, what he's buying. He takes another step forward and puts the box on the conveyor belt; then he looks up, maybe because he senses that someone is looking at him. His eyes move searchingly over the people. Meet Stella's gaze.

Mister Pfister looks at her.

Stella looks at Mister Pfister; she thinks, Can you feel that the entire way one person can take to approach another is encompassed in this look. The way there, and the way back too.

Anger, courtesy, plus something else.

Stella almost wants to smile. With a great effort she manages to control the childish impulse to smile that threatens to burst through. She almost wants to say hello; the moment of recognition is so powerful that it seems the gracious thing to do, Oh, we know each other, hello. But there's no need to greet Mister Pfister; he knows that she has recognised him, that she knows him. And he doesn't smile, not even a little bit. To be precise, he doesn't smile at all. Instead, he will wait. He will wait for her outside by the door, to begin what's been demanded all along here: a conversation.

Perhaps it will be easy; in spite of everything it might be easy in a way. Stella might say, Don't do it any more, you hear me. Do you understand, stop ringing the doorbell, all that mail; just stop coming by our house; give it up. Give up; that's how she could say it.

Stella breaks eye contact with Mister Pfister. It's possible he already broke eye contact with her earlier. How long were they looking at each other? No window, no garden gate, no fence separating them from each other.

Stella enters the supermarket through the turnstile; she doesn't turn around again. She buys milk, eggs, alphabet noodles, butter, the things she wanted to buy, nothing more, nothing less, but she is in more of a hurry than usual; she is rushing. She dashes through the aisles, feeling utterly tense, and by the time she turns around the last rack of shelves before the checkout counter, those for lemonade powder, chocolate and candy, in front of which Ava always wants to stand forever,

Mister Pfister is already gone. He has paid for his stuff – which Stella would have liked to see, knowing that Jason would find this curiosity of hers distasteful – and is already outside, he has already gone off. What is it that Stella actually wants to know, and how far can she stretch this question.

She puts her things down on the conveyor belt at the checkout. Her heart is beating more calmly now; even as she's counting her change she has an inkling of an impending disappointment.

Have a good evening.

You too.

The car park outside the supermarket is deserted. Stella's face is hot. Mister Pfister is nowhere in sight. Mister Pfister has lost his need, his fervent desire to speak to Stella. That's both hurtful and a relief. But why? Why doesn't he want to speak to Stella any more; what has changed, been lost. The long look between her and him becomes at first questionable and then humiliating. Stella puts her purchases into the basket on her bicycle. She thinks, Maybe I got even older these past weeks, and she has to laugh a little at that. She pushes her bike across the car park and Main Street, along Forest Lane, past the first houses of the development; she walks on the left side of the street and, as her house comes into view, the jasmine hedge, the fence, Jason's car in the driveway, the open dormer window, she sees Mister Pfister standing at her garden gate. She's still quite a distance away from the house, but she sees him clearly; he rings the bell, doesn't wait, turns away and calmly walks off at a measured pace, down the street towards his house.

Stella stands still, hands tightly gripping the handlebars of her bike. She can't believe it. Mister Pfister has rung the bell at her gate even though he knows that she isn't home. Apparently he also knows that Jason and Ava aren't home. Jason and Ava are at the children's party in the Community Centre. Stella baked a lemon cake for it and standing outside her house had waved after them until they were out of sight. Mister Pfister couldn't wait outside the shopping centre for Stella, but he has to stop outside her house; she can understand that as a tic, a compulsion; it's simply impossible for Mister Pfister to walk by her house without ringing the bell. No matter whether Stella is there or not. Doesn't give a damn. But she can also interpret it this way – There is no Stella. The Stella Mister Pfister has in mind doesn't exist; in any case, *she* has nothing to do with that Stella. Mister Pfister recognised her, but that's not who he's interested in – this Stella who goes shopping after work in flat-heeled sandals and with a tired face without make-up, tense, harried, and obviously needy, this Stella doesn't interest him. Mister Pfister is interested in Stella in her locked house. In her face behind the small windowpane next to the door, her distant figure in the chair at the edge of the lawn far back in the garden, in the Stella waiting at her desk upstairs in her room. That Stella is the one Mister Pfister is interested in. An imagined Stella. *His* Stella.

*

Stella realises that there's nothing she can do against this. She can't take this other Stella away from Mister Pfister.

She watches him walking away, his boyish figure; he's pulled the black hood over his head, it looks like a suit of armour. She rolls her bike slowly forward until he arrives at his own house, having passed all the houses she's now familiar with. She waits until he's disappeared into his garden, and she knows that he knows that she is watching him.

Fourteen

I'd like to show you something, Jason says.

He takes Stella by the hand and goes outside with her; hand in hand they walk to the garden gate; later Stella will think of this hand-in-hand as a betrayal. Jason opens the gate and steps with Stella out into the street. At the far end of the street a large flock of birds alights on the pavement. The wind is high up in the treetops, the pine trees at the edge of the forest creak. Stella feels an inordinately burdensome grief, a longing for another life or a life she once had; exactly which life she can't recall.

Jason's hand is dry and warm. It is the most familiar thing about Jason.

He stops in front of the garden gate, lets go of Stella and looks at her. She is supposed to see something that he saw long ago, something about this situation is like a déjà-vu. But Stella doesn't see it. Jason touches her shoulder, he turns her back around to face the house and waits; then he points at the mailbox; he points at it. On the mailbox, under Stella's and Jason's names, there is a third name written neatly and like theirs with a white grease pencil directly on the metal of the box, except in a different, a distinctive, feminine handwriting.

Mister Pfister.

Don't touch it, Jason says, quite superfluously.

He says, Do you have any idea how long that's been there? Can you somehow make sense of this?

Fifteen

Ava is sitting in the sandpit, talking to herself. She whispers, sternly shakes her head, with her tongue makes soft, clicking sounds that she must have heard from the aunties in the kindergarten. She has spread some objects out on the wooden board of the sandpit; she is offering them.

An apricot.

A little car.

A pen, a seashell, a shekel, a coin.

Ava pushes the objects on the board back and forth, she rearranges them; then she returns them to their original positions.

She says, You can buy the apricot, or you can take the shell. You can make a necklace for yourself with the shell. This here is a car. Papa's car from his childhood. A very old car. Old.

She puts the pail upside down on the board and the car on top of the pail. She gets out of the sandpit and walks over to the edge of the field, she looks at it and thinks it over thoroughly; then she snaps off a yarrow, a poppy and a chamomile flower, ties them together into a bristly bouquet, and puts the bouquet on the board next to the apricot.

She says pensively, I'm thirsty.

She says, Today at kindergarten there was a man nobody knew. Nobody knew him. He had on a black sweater with a hood, and he told me to say hello to you, Mama. I didn't say anything. Do we know him? Have you ever seen him?

Sixteen

When Stella picks up Esther and Walter's key from the office, Paloma, telephone receiver at her ear, signals to her to wait. She beckons with her index finger, indicating the chair in front of her desk.

Stella makes coffee while Paloma is telephoning. She listens to Paloma's unemotional, cool voice. If the family doesn't want to rely on the nursing staff, we have to end the relationship. You're underestimating your mother. You underestimate your mother's abilities, the mental faculties of elderly people in general.

Paloma listens to the voice on the receiver with a nasty smile. The kettle rumbles and switches off. The smell of the instant coffee is delicious and artificial, reminding Stella unfailingly of campsites, nights in tents, waking up by the ocean; it never and will not later ever remind her of Paloma's office, of the postcards above Paloma's desk, or of the static stillness of those years.

She takes a mug with a tiger on it for herself and one with the words *destroy something* on it for Paloma. She waits, then pours water over the two teaspoons of coffee, stirs some coffee whitener into each, then places Paloma's mug next to the phone.

Paloma says, Think it over. Best wishes for the time being; please get in touch once you've made your decision; she makes a horrible grimace, puts the receiver back and turns to Stella. She says abruptly, This morning there was a man here. Standing outside the office when I arrived; could be he'd already been waiting for a while. He asked about personnel. About a nurse for his mother. He asked about you.

What did you say, Stella says. She feels as if she's falling, falling forward, towards Paloma.

Well, he asked for your phone number, Paloma says slowly. To contact you; he wanted your number.

Paloma looks at Stella for a long time. Then she says, Of course I didn't give it to him. I said I was in charge of making arrangements. He can't choose his own personnel here anyway.

Yes, Stella says.

Paloma says, Stella, I'm not sure. That was a pretty weird sort of guy, and he didn't look like someone who'd be worried about his sick mother. To be frank, he looked deranged. I told him we were fully booked. We had no available staff. A young man in a black hooded sweater, good-looking actually. But all done in. Do you know who that could have been?

No, Stella says. Don't know, no idea.

She has to get out of there before she starts to cry; she really has to see to it that she can get out of there, disappear.

She says, OK, Paloma. I've got to go now. Esther is waiting. I've got to go. I'll come back later. Maybe you'll still be here then.

I'll still be here, Paloma says. Of course I'll still be here then. Why did you make coffee for yourself if you have to leave right away. You're as white as a sheet, Stella. What's the matter with you?

Seventeen

Stella tries not to think about Mister Pfister. She tries to do away with him by not thinking of him, to get him out of her house by not thinking about him. It's impossible.

She wakes at daybreak; the coordinates of the days intrude into her half-sleep.

Ava.

The house in the development on the outskirts of the city, the room under the roof, the bed with the window on the right, the not-quite closed door on the left, and on the other side of the door, the hall, Ava's room, Ava.

Jason. Present, his slender form next to her in bed so surprisingly slight in sleep; Jason's absence, Jason rather far away, and the bed next to Stella is empty.

Time of day, morning around six, and the season, summer.
The window is open; many diverse and wary bird voices.
And Mister Pfister. Still there.

Stella turns on her side and imagines Mister Pfister waking
up. He wakes up in his room next to the kitchen. She is sure he
doesn't use all the rooms in his house, that the many rooms in his
house are too much of a challenge for him. He'll keep the doors
to them closed, possibly locked; he'll only rarely go upstairs to
the first floor. He has retreated to the room next to the kitchen,
the room that corresponds to Stella and Jason's living room.
The room is dark because the picture window is draped with
black felt. Mister Pfister isn't awakened by daylight and wakes
up at all sorts of times, sometimes at dawn, sometimes during
the night, also in the afternoon or early evening. Time, Stella
thinks, is relative for Mister Pfister. It is dark when he wakes
up, or it is bright, it is dawn turning into day or already dusk
turning back to night; it rains, snows, then the sun rises.

For Mister Pfister time is different, it ticks differently; Stella's time is what determines Mister Pfister's time. If Stella's time
didn't exist, and Ava's and Jason's – then there would be a different one for him. Mister Pfister wakes up and lies there, simply
lies there with closed eyes, and at six o'clock in the morning he
hears exactly the same things as Stella – birds, the distant noise
of traffic, the slamming of car doors – yet under or maybe over
it, he hears something completely different, a mesh, a web of
voices that Stella can't hear, a disembodied whispering.

Then he gets up.

Stella sees Mister Pfister getting up and going into the kitchen
and turning on the kettle. He rolls himself a cigarette while he
waits for the water to boil. The kitchen is only dimly lit. There's

quite a lot of paper on the floor; in a bowl in the corner by the window onions are sending glowing green shoots up into the air like flames; there are far too many bottles in this kitchen, beer bottles, wine bottles, pickle jars, and piles of paper under which the essential things – pens, packets of tobacco, lighters, notes, viewpoints and thoughts – get lost; but they'll all turn up again, no need to worry about that. Nothing gets lost; it all goes around in a circle.

The water is boiling. Mister Pfister pours hot water on top of a large spoonful of coffee in a dirty mug; the image of the dirty mug fills Stella with satisfaction. He drinks his coffee black, without milk and without sugar. What does the aroma of coffee in the morning remind Mister Pfister of; I don't even want to know, Stella thinks; I really don't want to know.

Mister Pfister opens a beer to go with his coffee. He finds one among all the empty bottles; there's always one last beer still there. The cigarette crackles extravagantly. Everything is hot and cold at the same time, light and dark, soft and loud. And paper is scattered everywhere. Paper spreads from the kitchen into the living room, crunched-up paper, paper densely covered with writing, graph paper from school notebooks in the midst of stacks of newspapers, notebooks, boxes, piles of wrapping paper, advertisements and cardboard; but Mister Pfister strides through it all as if over water, he strides back to the living room and only now turns on the music, frees up the room – it's Bach.

It's all you can hear.

Stella has never before heard Bach. Not knowingly heard Bach, not this way. She decides never to listen to Bach. Never.

Mister Pfister searches for an ashtray. He crawls around the room on all fours and finds a plastic ashtray. The coffee is

pitch black; the music will be clear as glass. Mister Pfister has to
drink a second beer immediately. He is ill too, he feels ill, tired,
exhausted. To listen. To lie down, to listen lying down, and
rummaging from his bed among the papers, to find a pencil and
write down something, compulsively write something down,
namely three words:

Emergency, memory, light.

All of them words that beat their wings, Stella thinks. Maybe
it feels as if, by writing them down, they will keep still – *Resistance, presence of mind, ward, thirty-seven, Monday, back then.*
It isn't as if these were merely ugly words, dull, blunt words.
They are words that might be an announcement, an excessive
demand. Or just an invitation?

Transitions. Dogs. Despair.

Mister Pfister's pencil scribbles and scratches across the crumpled paper and breaks. Now and then Mister Pfister is carried
along on a wave of self-assurance, of arrogance and glaring confidence. A third beer. There's also always a third beer, and the
atmosphere clinks among all the bottles. Mister Pfister ought to
eat something. But before that he has to lie down again; perhaps
he'll fall asleep again, and when he wakes up for the third time,
there suddenly, on the floor next to his bed is an alarm clock; it's
already afternoon, high time; the alarm clock ticks deafeningly,
each second a detonation. Mister Pfister gets up at once and gets
dressed. Trousers, hooded sweater, trainers. He fumbles in the
pile of stuff and crud on the kitchen table; a photo slides out of the
pile, in it he's sitting on the edge of a bed in a room at a completely
different time; he absolutely has to get rid of this photo; this photo
can't remain in the system for a moment longer; it's got to go.

Mister Pfister puts the photo in his pocket.

Leaves his house.

Carefully double-locks the door, locks the garden gate.

He walks past the bicycle mechanic's house. The bicycle mechanic is sitting in front of his door on a folding chair as he does every day; the wheel he's holding turns, releasing sparks; the sparks fly into the dark, warm day. This bicycle mechanic belongs to Mister Pfister. Everything about the house, the small workshop, the bikes, the golden sparks, the light and the friendliness belong to Mister Pfister; later on he'll say this to Stella just like that – you were just speaking to my bicycle mechanic, and you'll be punished for that. Punished. That's how he'll say it. He walks along the street past the house with the awning; the awning is drawn up, not that this would interest Mister Pfister, none of it interests Mister Pfister at all. He walks past the silent gardens, and at the end of the street Stella comes around the corner; she's coming; she's already there.

Mister Pfister steps out of the way onto the fallow land, the empty lot. He stumbles off towards the right, onto rubble and debris.

Stella gets off her bike. There are two bags hanging from the handlebars. That child is sitting in a child's seat, pointing here and there. Stella leans the bike against the garden fence, puts the bags down, lifts that child out of the seat and hands her the keys; the child unlocks the gate with a lot of fuss and disappears into the garden. Stella pushes the bike along behind her; comes back to get the bags, and only now, only now, she glances down the street in the direction of Mister Pfister's house. But Mister Pfister has just stepped to one side; actually he doesn't give a damn, doesn't give a damn, whether she sees him or not; that's not what it's all about at all, that's not what it's about.

A blazing look.
Supper, Friday.
Mister Pfister stands with his hands in his trouser pockets, waiting. Behind him in the shrubbery on the fallow land, the nightingales are beginning to sing.

Lighthouses. Morse code. Quite clearly the arcs are beginning to come together, to close. These and those. Mister Pfister's feelings vacillate between hate and love, anger and confidence; this is quite normal, it happens to everybody; it really happens to everybody; he can be quite sure on that score.

And then it's evening.

In Stella's house, in the many rooms in which she lives and thinks and sleeps and eats and talks with her people, the back door to the garden opens. That child comes walking out.

Well then, let's go. Let's go.

And Mister Pfister pushes off and gets going. Towards Stella's house; he stops at the garden gate, puts a finger on the bell below which on the mailbox is her name, and under her name is his: Mister Pfister; and he presses the bell as hard as he can.

He takes a step back and looks at the house. For the thousandth time. The house is exactly the same house as his. There's no one in the living room. The dormer window is open, the orange flag is waving from it. The child has gone into hiding. The garden is wild and very luxuriant. Stella's predilection for mullein, lupines, unmown grass, for shells, stones, the child's fondness for little sticks and junk.

Mister Pfister listens. He listens a moment longer, stands there another moment among the atmospheric shards, Stella, the bike, the child's little hat, the little cherry-red dress, the paper bags, the sentences spoken between Stella and this child, words, gestures, handing over the keys, the touching, then he steps forward.

Mister Pfister kicks open the garden gate; for the very first time he simply goes ahead and does that now. The gate yields, opens up, swings on its hinges, and the garden at last becomes large and bright; it was, after all, high time. Mister Pfister takes the photo out of his trouser pocket, the gruesome, wrinkled photo of the bed in the room, *back then*, and he opens the mailbox and drops the photo into it, as matter-of-factly as if into a fathoms-deep well, how else, for bloody damn sake.

Nobody in sight.

Somewhere water is dripping.

Tomorrow they'll meet again.

Mister Pfister goes, leaving something behind. He goes to the right or the left, depending, there are no rules, only a few rules; the rules here are made some place else.

*

And Stella turns in her bed and sits up. The entire room smells of forest, of pines and sand. She sits on the edge of her bed, hands between her knees like Dermot on a boulder by the water forty years ago, and she looks out of the open window up into the morning sky. This is not the way she'll be able to kill Mister Pfister. This image will keep him alive for sure. The thought is onerous and disgusting, and Stella feels compassion and the opposite of compassion, but she can't get away from the image; it's her way of defending herself. The pictures come from books she's read, the memories of people she's known, and from herself, from Stella alone; it could be that none of all this has anything to do with reality. That Mister Pfister is an entirely different person, possibly someone who isn't sick or is sick in a different way than she imagines; what actually does the image she has formed of him say about her? It's possible that Mister Pfister doesn't touch even a drop of alcohol. That he telephones his girlfriend every evening, sitting erect at a neat desk in a clean room, and that Stella's image of him is naïve. Stupid. But aren't they alike then, Stella and Mister Pfister? Isn't this something that connects them to each other, in spite of everything.

*

Dreams, like the shedding of skins.

Eighteen

Stella takes her bike to the back of the house. She twists off the valve cap, listens to the air escaping, waits a while. Then she closes the valve again, puts the cap on the windowsill and pushes the bike out of the garden.

*

The bicycle mechanic is sitting in the afternoon sun in front of his house on a folding chair next to a little table. He's drinking tea out of a chipped cup, has just rolled himself a cigarette but not yet lit it. He's wearing a shirt that's been mended in many places the old-fashioned way, dirty trousers and sturdy shoes. Next to him, dusty bikes leaning against each other next to the house wall. The picture windowpane is turned green by the large plants clustered behind it.

Would you like a cup of tea.

He's not at all surprised by Stella's arrival. Points at the bikes leaning against each other; she adds her bike to them. He goes around the corner of the house, comes back with a second chair, and unfolds it next to his own. He says, Actually, it's nicer to sit out back, but you know that already. Then he disappears into the house.

Stella sits down.

Tobacco, cigarette papers, an ashtray, an address book, a box of matches with a carnation on top, and a book without a dust jacket whose spine Stella can't decipher, and which she doesn't have the nerve to turn over, are lying on the little table. She hears the bicycle mechanic walking around inside the house, clattering in the kitchen; it's odd to know where the kitchen is in his house; it's also peculiar to sit outside his house, looking out at the familiar yet at the same time different street. The gate is wide open. Dandelions and wild mint grow in the rubble next to the fence. Water for the flowers in plastic bottles. A rusted tank between his property and Mister Pfister's. The grass around Mister Pfister's house is dry. His house looks deserted, downright grey.

The bicycle mechanic puts a cup of tea on the little table next to Stella. The tea is clear and golden; this cup too has a crack. The bicycle mechanic sits down on the second chair. They sit next to each other, looking out at the street where a hunchbacked, sharp-eyed child is pushing a scooter past the gate from right to left as if on cue.

I work here just for myself, the bicycle mechanic says. This isn't an official workshop; I work on my own.

I know, Stella says. I thought as much.

He nods. He says, Your child goes to the Community

Kindergarten, and you always disappear into the Community Centre. Do you work in the Community Centre.

I pick up keys there, Stella says. At the office for Home Nursing Care. The office is in the Community Centre, and I pick up the keys to my patients' homes there. I'm a nurse. I work for Paloma.

They talk a little together. They try to have a conversation, what Mister Pfister had asked for and Stella had refused him. She's talking with this bicycle mechanic who of course reminds her of Jason – dirty hands, black, lively eyes, a quiet physical tension, and a dangerous politeness; where does that come from, and what does it mean. They talk a little about the belated spring, everything in bloom at the same time, lilac, horse chestnuts, a phenomenon. About winter, which the bicycle mechanic spends in the South because he can't stand the freezing cold, not coming back until the days get longer again. About the old development; he says that he would leave as soon as the exalted pretensions of the new development cross the street. He speaks slowly, almost sleepily, yet precisely.

There is a time warp here, have you noticed that already? Time has stood still here, and everyone who lives here keeps to himself. I've seen you for years, yet this is the first time we're talking to each other. There are scarcely any changes. This is not an open neighbourhood, but for a while that can be a good thing, a necessary thing maybe.

He looks at Stella thoughtfully. Then he says, Do you dance.

No, Stella says. I never dance.

It feels funny to say that sentence. I never dance. She thinks, Sometimes I dance with Esther, and she has to laugh at that; he laughs too, laughs to himself in a knowing way.

I'm sure you'd be a good tango dancer.

Unlikely, Stella thinks, that certain things will still happen. That I'll dance at some time or other. And is that too bad, or isn't it.

She raises her cup and extends her legs. The bicycle mechanic's wristwatch emits a soft signal tone, four o'clock; he says, I set it once by accident, and I've left it like that ever since. It's certainly not supposed to remind me that it's the end of the work day. All I can do is ask myself what happened on this day, that's all.

And what happened today, Stella asks hesitantly.

I repaired a bike. Read one page in a book, watered my plants, you came by, and I made tea for you. Definitely a lot for one day.

*

At some point Stella says it.

I wanted to ask you about Mister Pfister, about your neighbour. I wanted to ask you whether you know him.

She says it, then holds her breath.

Of course I know Mister Pfister, the bicycle mechanic says. He says it without making a face, doesn't bat an eye. I know pretty much all the people living on this street. Except for you, probably. All of them except for you.

He says, Why do you ask? What do you want to know?

Stella sits up in her chair, exhales, and leans forward. She is filled with regret; she feels reminded of something, almost, something from her childhood, something long forgotten.

She wants to know whether the matter is getting out of hand. But how is the bicycle mechanic concerned in that?

Stella says, The thing is, Mister Pfister wants to talk to me. It's that he'd like to have a conversation with me.

Yes, and what's so hard about that? the bicycle mechanic says with a smile, and what is he supposed to say, after all; so of course he asks exactly this stupid and appropriate question.

Yes but I don't want to, Stella says. I don't want to have a conversation with him, and he can't understand that. He simply doesn't understand; he won't leave me alone; he is terrorising me. He's terrorising me. Her voice is trembling audibly.

The bicycle mechanic looks out into the street. Not over towards Mister Pfister's.

He says, All right, when the sun goes down, we'll go to the back of the house.

Thank you very much, Stella says.

She waits a while. Then she says, What kind of person is he. Can you tell me something about him, would that be possible.

The bicycle mechanic could say, Why should I of all people tell you about Mister Pfister. He could say, Why me, I'm not getting involved in that. But that isn't what he does. He comes to Stella's aid; at least he speaks, doesn't refuse to give her an answer. In doing so he reveals a little about himself. We do that all the time, Stella thinks, gratefully; we keep revealing ourselves.

The bicycle mechanic says, Mister Pfister comes over to visit me sometimes. He sits there where you're sitting now. He's pretty alone. I can imagine quite well that he can't accept a No, he's out of practice; he doesn't have much to do with other people. Maybe it's always been like that. Could be.

He says, Mister Pfister used to be good-looking – not any more; he takes medications, there are mental problems. He could have had several women, but didn't. In spite of that he's very full of himself, that's obvious. He thinks he's fine. He has a high opinion of himself; he's smug and conceited too. When we sit here together, he likes to tell me things. Knows what's going on. What keeps the world from coming apart; he has his own ideas about what's going on. Dead sure. Not open to other opinions, you might say. Mister Pfister is not open to other ideas.

He finally lights his cigarette, inhales once, twice, and then looks briefly over at Mister Pfister's house, not worried, rather as if he wanted to check on something. Then he says, But he's also touchy. Sensitive, educated; at some point he must have wanted something. If he follows you, he's probably not doing well. I haven't seen him for quite a while. It's been quite a while since he's come over; who knows what that may mean.

He doesn't follow me, Stella says. He harasses me; there's a difference. I'd like him to stop. I can't stand it any more.

Then you have to tell him that; the bicycle mechanic looks at Stella impassively; he seems to be wondering which side he'd be on if someone were to ask him. It's obvious he isn't necessarily Mister Pfister's friend, but he seems to like him.

Tell him that. If you've never spoken to him, then maybe you ought to do it sometime. Tell him, talk to him. One can talk to him; I'm sure one can.

Oh, Stella says. Can one?

This suggestion is the opposite of Jason's advice. The opposite of Clara's advice, all the advice in the goddamn miserable network. But Stella senses that she's going to listen to this suggestion. What would Jason and Clara say? And what would they say about her even sitting here.

But after all she isn't sitting here secretly. Jason can walk by the house; Mister Pfister can walk by the house; anybody can.

Let's move to another spot, the bicycle mechanic says, move into the warm setting sun.

He takes his cup off the table and pours the rest of the tea into the grass with a conclusive or preparatory gesture.

Yes, Stella says. With pleasure.

Could I go through the house? Through the hall and the kitchen, out the back; I'd like to see what your house looks like. Compared to mine.

Of course, the bicycle mechanic says. Of course you can.

He gets up before she does and goes in ahead of her.

Nineteen

These days Esther does everything by herself. When Stella arrives, she's already sitting in the kitchen. She has dressed herself, straightened her bed, put her medication, glasses, pencils, crossword puzzles and newspaper on the tray of her walker and set off. She has closed the kitchen door, which at other times is left wide open, behind her; Stella assumes this is supposed to mean something, but can't imagine what. Esther is sitting at the kitchen table and has the radio on very loud. She's listening to a classical music concert and raises her hand in warning when Stella enters the kitchen. In spite of that Stella starts to unpack her purchases, wash the dishes, sweep up. You have no idea, Esther says; it's really astonishing that you don't have the slightest inkling about anything.

She inclines her head to the radio and conducts an invisible orchestra with skilful little gestures. Pa-ti-ta. Pa-ti-ta. Pa-ti – listen, now here they are. The mermaids. Esther shakes her head and gestures as if Stella had said something, then she turns the radio off and bends over the television listings, and with angry strokes checks all the programmes she wants to watch, that she considers worthwhile.

I can take care of myself. Please make me some toast with orange marmalade since you're sneaking around here anyway, and sweep the room, the dust balls are as big as a child's head; I wonder where you learned to keep house. You're pale. You should change your hairstyle. You ought to see more people; I think I'm the only person you have anything to do with.

Stella empties the commode, the washbowl, the mug with Esther's stringy spit, she rinses the mug at the sink in the bathroom looking elsewhere, certainly not in the mirror. She vacuums, piles up the old newspapers; she's brought along flowers, irises and roses, and she arranges them carefully in Esther's glass vase; she listens to Esther's monologues and thinks there is a kernel of truth in what Esther's going on about. Esther is not well liked. Stella puts the books Esther has dropped behind the bed over the weekend back on the shelf. Volumes of poetry, short stories, dream interpretations. She wipes off the shelf and arranges the photos of Esther's children and grand-children again; it's sad to see how many people Esther has lived with, and how alone she now is. Get down to business, Esther calls from the kitchen. Get a move on! She doesn't specify what business, what move she's referring to.

Stella sits down at the table with Esther; cuts the toast into small pieces, says, Esther, be sensible. Let me get at your ear to measure your blood sugar. Esther turns and with the expression of an offended child that knows better, holds her left ear to Stella. Stella squeezes a drop of blood from the soft, delicate earlobe. Your sugar is too high, Esther; and then she watches as Esther confidently lifts her shirt and injects insulin into her swollen abdomen. She records Esther's numbers in the record book; they sit together peacefully. Stella has the clear sense that Esther is glad she is there, even though she would never say so. In suspiciously good shape, the night nurse had written into the record book, conspicuously lively. Stella knows what that means; increased vitality is often followed by illness, a fall or an accident.

Close that awful book, Esther says sternly. Leave now. There's a fresh wind blowing here, I can feel it, and the two of us, you and I, we won't be seeing much of each other any more. How is your child?

She's well, Stella says. She's doing well. Last week she lost both of her front teeth at the same time; she looks like a little vampire.

Aha. Esther smiles vaguely. She says, I think you'll be leaving us, or am I mistaken. You'll put a nice letter of resignation on Paloma's desk, that's what you'll do. Am I wrong.

No, Stella says. She says, I don't know.

Well, Esther says, this is a dead corner. A dead corner of the world. I don't remember any more what brought me here, how in God's name I ever came to be here.

Stella ponders this as she gets on her bicycle outside Esther's house. She could have said, Same here. I don't remember either what brought me here, how I got here.

In the dim summery light the gardens disappear, the ordinary streets suddenly look completely foreign to her; something is changing, has already changed.

*

Recently, Stella writes to Clara, *I've been having the same dreams I had when I was a child. I dream about the doll's house that stood in my nursery and a tiny little being, which I know is evil, flits through the night-time doll's house. It hides in the doll's house; it's not to be found, but I know it's there; it's in my house. What does this mean? I'm writing you this letter sitting in the garden, it's already almost dark; I can't see what I put down on the paper, and I don't have any words either, not a single little word for my longing for Jason, that feels so final, as if he were dead. But he isn't dead. He'll come back again tomorrow, and three beers and a bowl of plums are waiting for him in the refrigerator. Do you still remember how full of confidence we were ten years ago? Almost reckless. And yet it was all about nothing. What we wanted is what we have – a husband, child, a roof over our head, a self-contained life. It's going to rain soon; you can feel it before it really starts to rain; it's something electric, it's in the air. Clara, Take care. As ever your –*

*

Heat hangs over the city; at night the horizon doesn't turn black any more, but glows ominously and threateningly orange from under a bank of clouds. Contrary to Paloma's pronouncement no one dies, but the nursing shifts are arduous and exhausting. Stella accompanies Walter to the hospital. Walter's catheter has to be exchanged; he has to have his bowel irrigated and then undergo a colonoscopy. He'll have to stay in the hospital for one long, hot week, and Stella doesn't know whether Walter knows that his family is coming this week to talk to Paloma; his sisters and his brother. Possibly they'll take him to a nursing home, clean out and sell his house; how do you transport those fragile cardboard models of bridges, and will it even matter to anyone. Who will take care of the canaries. Could the canaries, if they were freed, survive in the suburban gardens? Stella sits next to Walter in the ambulette. Walter is buckled into his wheelchair; the windows of the ambulette are made of frosted glass, they can't be opened; it's impossible to find out what section of town they're in, where they are. Walter can't even look out of the window, now that he is actually being driven through the city. Ava would break out in tears at this injustice. There's a traffic jam. The tinted glass pane separating them from the driver's compartment is closed, and Stella and Walter watch the inaudible conversation of the drivers, which is apparently about all those things that have always been and will never change, a choreography of gestures and head shaking. They are stuck in the traffic jam. Walter closes his eyes. He turns his face to Stella as if for a very last look, a face from the series of sleepers hanging above his bed. What is Walter dreaming about. Stella knows so much about him and yet so little. She looks at him. In a sickly way he is carefully shaved and his eyelids are wrinkled; the eyelashes are thick as a child's. He opens his eyes again as if Stella had seen enough. He says, Thirsty, and Stella lifts up the cup and puts the straw between his lips, wipes the water from his chin with a cloth, and puts the cup down again. She says, Is that enough. Walter doesn't answer. The driver brakes, finally stops, and turns off the engine. Stella sees from Walter's smile that he doesn't care, that there's no connection between things anyway.

She had spent the morning with him at his desk, lifting his

heavy arms and legs, saying, Contract, Walter, do it yourself, contract your muscles, and Walter wasn't able to complete even one coordinated movement. Should we stop? But he had shaken his head, apparently wanting to go on, to endure it, this sweaty work together in the middle of the living room in the oppressive heat, in front of the television, in front of the animated cartoons, as if the odd movements of the cartoon figures were more like Walter's own movements than any single movement in real life.

Stella leans forward and taps on the glass divider; the driver turns around and opens the glass a crack, a prison guard would do it no differently.

Do you have any idea, Stella says not concentrating; I mean, can you estimate how long we'll have to stand here like this; because if it's going to be a long time, we would get out. She knows she sounds like a wilful child.

Freedom. The freedom to get out of a car.

If I knew stuff like that, the driver says, I wouldn't be sitting here. I'd be somewhere else, somewhere completely different, and he leaves it at this arbitrary answer, shuts the divider, turns away.

I'm going to be leaving, Walter, Stella says. She crumples the damp cloth in her lap. I wanted you to know. I'm going to stop working for Paloma; we're moving. I'll still be here till the end of the month; then I'll hand in my notice; I'm not sure when Paloma can let me go. I'll still be here when you come back from the hospital. In any case. But later on I'll have to leave.

She talks and talks. She knows that she's talking like this because Walter won't be saying anything in reply. Can't say anything about it and can't ask any questions; he can only alternate between syllables, between sounds that can be understood one way or another, depending, depending on what Stella wants to hear.

*

Dermot says, What did you eat today?

What did I eat today, Stella says. She has to think about it for a moment, then she remembers – lettuce. I ate lettuce and bread and the last cold pancake that Ava couldn't manage to eat yesterday. And you?

A little bit of soup, Dermot says absent-mindedly. It's actually too hot to eat, isn't it. But one has to eat. One has to eat something.

Why did you ask what I ate, Stella asks in all seriousness.

Sometimes that can be a distraction, Dermot says, and he smiles as if she'd caught him at something.

They're standing together in Dermot's garden. Julia is in the hospital. She'd got up during the night, had sat down in the kitchen, waiting for a sign, and had finally left the house at dawn; she fell just outside the house, and Dermot found her on the front stairs. She was dressed as if for a Sunday church service or for a concert; blood was coming out of her ears. Where did she get the strength to do this, and why didn't Dermot hear her; why didn't he hear her get up. How is that possible. Stella thinks that in a certain way Julia walked out of the picture. Walked out for good; a move she had begun by the sea in March forty years ago and had now completed.

It seems, Dermot says casually, that we'll be packing our things at the same time. You and I. Our, how do you say it – our trash. He looks at Stella, his face is too familiar for her to be able to tell how sad he is. His friendliness seems to have faded, warmth diminishing, withdrawing. Stella thinks she can understand that.

He jerks his large head as if he wanted to keep her from such thoughts. He says, Do you already know what you want to do?

No, Stella says. She has to smile; it's embarrassing not to know what she wants to do. She says, The sort of work I do I can do anywhere, can't I. I mean, there are people everywhere like you, like Julia, like Esther. There are people everywhere like Paloma. But perhaps I'll do something completely different. Let's wait and see?

Yes. You'll see, Dermot says. He sounds matter-of-fact. Change releases energy, an energy you perhaps don't even know of yet.

Stella thinks, But that also applies to you then. Does that also apply to you? Will Julia's death release an energy in you which you don't have any inkling of now; what energy is that supposed to be.

She can't imagine. She stands next to Dermot, and they watch the wind blow through the tarpaulins outside the house. The tarps ripple in a wave-like motion like water, reflecting the light.

Twenty

At midday, after Jason's departure, Mister Pfister puts a yellow slip of paper into the mailbox.

Stella sees him coming from the bedroom – she is straightening up the bureau, sorting Jason's shirts, extending his presence that way; she doesn't want to lose touch – she sees Mister Pfister walking down the street, hoodie top, dark trousers, swollen face, left hand in his trouser pocket; he stuffs what he has in his right hand directly into the mailbox. Then he presses the bell, looking up towards the bedroom, leaving his thumb on the bell while looking up.

Stella, upstairs in the bedroom, looks down at him. The bell shrills. She stands at the open window with Jason's shirts in her arms looking down at Mister Pfister; he stands, as if framed by the window, the mullein on the left, the edge of the forest on the right, what a picture. Then the bell stops ringing. Mister Pfister turns and walks back home.

*

Stella finishes sorting the laundry. She makes the bed, partially closes the window. In the kitchen she puts the breakfast dishes into the sink and shakes the tea leaves out of the teapot; she neatly folds up the newspaper Jason read that morning, looking for a while at the photo above the headline: three Chinese astronauts who have landed on a desolate landscape. Carefully she wipes off the kitchen table, just can't stop wiping the kitchen table. She goes into the hall and lets down her hair in front of the mirror, combing it and pinning it together again. She pinches her cheeks, the way Clara always used to. Clara always did that. She puts on her jacket, locks the front door behind her, and unlocks the mailbox.

*

Hello, so what does it feel like to be stalked

*

Stella closes the mailbox without touching the piece of paper. She leaves the garden and walks out into the warm day, turning left down the street, in Mister Pfister's violently vibrating tracks. The house of the female student, that of the Asian family, that of the old woman, her deserted garden, the pruned rhododendron, a garden umbrella at the edge of the field, open above an overturned chair. The fallow land of the empty lot, poplar pollen in the gutter, dandelions, then the pool, the terrace where a man sitting in the shade turns disinterestedly to watch Stella, and at last the familiar, fairy-tale house of the bicycle mechanic, a house made of glass, the smell of which Stella knows once and for all – linen and curd soap and mint; she knows how the light falls onto the tiles in the room under the roof and that there are things standing on the stairs for which no place has yet been found, a wooden coffee grinder, juice glasses, film spools; she knows that there's a picture of a dog hanging on the wall between the living room and the kitchen and that the bicycle mechanic prefers green army jackets – his house is quiet. The two folding chairs lean against the wall, and the first of the bicycles next to the door is still hers.

Stella looks at the place in passing. She doesn't stop, doesn't really slow down; she arrives in front of Mister Pfister's house, locked gate and black windowpanes, nothing in the garden that would say anything about Mister Pfister, no twist in the plot.

Stella rings.

She can hear the bell shrilling inside the house, a bell like her own; still, it sounds different, a bit muted, muffled. She realises with surprise that Mister Pfister has actually got her to do exactly what *he* usually does – ringing the bell at a house where they don't want to open the door for her. Pressing her finger down hard on a bell in anger and fury and thinking, I know you're there.

He's managed to turn Stella into a mirror image of himself; so it would seem.

Stella says, she hisses: Come on out. Open the door. Open-the-door. Come on out.

The intercom crackles and she can hear his voice.

This is a private home.

Stella has to laugh at that. She makes a face, leans forward and says, Oh, yes, I know. Damn-it-all, I know that. And I don't even want to go inside your house. I would like to talk to you; open the goddamn door, open it.

Mister Pfister presses the buzzer. Stella leans against the gate; the gate opens. At the same time the front door opens, and Mister Pfister comes out. Stella sees him step onto the doorsill, and she has the feeling that with the opening of the door a sort of energy escapes the house like a liquid, a stream of thoughts and apprehensions, excess tension, oxidising fear. Mister Pfister looks as if it were the first time in his life he ever opened the door for someone. Walked towards someone, into the brightness, into the light. He sets his feet down like a sick person, just like Walter, Esther, Julia; he comes down the three steps towards Stella, a person who doesn't trust the ground under his feet. The air is thick. Stella feels she's starting to perspire; she can hear herself breathe. But her hands are ice cold; her mouth is dry; she visualises Ava, Ava's soft face, and she can hear her little hoarse voice; she also hears the voice of the bicycle mechanic, You can talk to him, go and talk to him.

Mister Pfister, as far as she can see, isn't holding anything. He comes towards her with empty hands. He makes a helpless, unambiguous gesture, he gestures at his door – he is inviting her in.

He is inviting her to come into his house, to sit down. To see what his house looks like compared to hers.

He has come outside for Stella; she has got him outside; is it possible, Stella thinks vaguely, that this was what it was all about for him. Again she sees how good-looking he is, how

young, and how tired; his face is ashen grey; the expression in
his eyes is desperate; he exudes a stale, sour smell; his mouth is
childish and much too large. He grimaces; maybe it's supposed
to be a smile. He is attempting something, trying to find a tone,
something he can hold on to.

Stella thinks of Jason. On the airplane, of his open hand; she
hears herself say, I have a fear of flying. I'm really very afraid of
flying, and she hears Jason's voice, his reassurance.

She shakes her head. I don't want to go inside your house.
And I don't want to stay long. You asked me a question; I want
to answer your question.

Mister Pfister stands still. Stella continues to walk towards
him; she could touch him, the dirty material of his hooded
sweater; make sure that he really exists. His expression changes
from desperation to confusion, then to a questioning lack of
understanding.

The piece of paper, Stella says. She spits out the words. Your
yellow, filthy piece of paper with the question, What is it like
being stalked. Yes?

Mister Pfister nods, it dawns on him, he retraces things. The
piece of paper. The question, the preclusion of a conversation,
his obsession, piecemeal things seem to occur to him, fragments;
he looks as if someone whom Stella can't see were whispering
something into his ear.

It's horrible being stalked. It's wrecking my life. It's wrecking me. I want you to stop it. I want you never again to ring the
bell at our house, never again to put anything into our mailbox;
I want you to get lost, once and for all. Do you understand. Do
you hear me?

It's a bit like talking to Ava. Somewhat like saying to Ava,

You have to keep your hat on your head. You should never cross the street when the light is red. It's high time you went to sleep now. Do you hear me. Are you listening to me?

Stella has a feeling of incipient nausea; maybe it's pity; it almost makes her stumble. Why doesn't she sit down with him on the steps in front of the house, one cigarette-length of time, just for a quarter of an hour, how hard would that be. She can't. No, she can't do it.

I just want to talk to someone, Mister Pfister says. He has trouble saying the words, difficulty pronouncing them, word by word, actually unconnected. To talk with somebody. I didn't know. I didn't know that it is terrible for you.

It is. It's terrible. And I'm not the right person, Stella says gently. She says it almost affectionately. You have to understand that I'm not the right person for that. You have to find someone else; we have nothing to do with each other; don't you see that? I'm not the person you think I am. I'm a completely different one.

How odd to say – but I'm not the right one. Simply to reject the look of another person. How do I know, Stella thinks, that I'm not the right one; where did I get that from.

They stand facing each other, looking at each other; Stella looks at Mister Pfister; she can see him, she'll never forget him. His green eyes, a yellow circle around the shaded iris, and behind the weariness, concealed amusement. His large mouth, a sickle-shaped scar on his upper lip, an expression of being overtaxed and at the same time knowing better. His posture, the total opposite of Jason's posture, of the bicycle mechanic's, his limp, tormented aura.

He extends his right hand. Chapped skin, flaky, incapable of squeezing something tight, of holding on to something. Stella raises her hands; she shows him her palms; it is impossible. Her hands. Good Lord. He pulls his hand back.

I wish you well.

Stella turns around. She sees the gate slamming shut before her, but that's only an illusory sequence, a panicky image, the gate is open and she walks through it and back out to the street, pulling the gate shut behind her without turning around again. She is trembling; everything is trembling.

*

Mister Pfister comes by that afternoon.

Did she assume he wouldn't come any more? Did she seriously think the matter was finished, that she could turn to other things (a page in a book, a poem, the magazine section of the Sunday paper, harvesting raspberries, cleaning windows); did she think she had done everything right.

She hadn't.

Mister Pfister rings that afternoon at three o'clock, and Stella gets up out of her chair behind the house, and not taking the time to put her shoes back on, she walks barefoot across the lawn and towards the gate, towards Mister Pfister, she runs. He's standing there, waiting for her, looking towards her. The bicycle mechanic was wrong.

Stella follows the *House Rules*. She lets anyone in, whoever-may-come. She pulls open the gate, Mister Pfister is not shocked by this, but he does take a small step back, only a small step, and without averting his fervent gaze from Stella's face.

Stella says, You can't leave it alone. It isn't possible, or what. Impossible for you, or what. She has the feeling that she is white with rage. She feels she can't see properly; all the contours are much too precise, they hurt her eyes.

Mister Pfister says, No, no, not possible. It's impossible, I can't let it be. Can't let it be.

He is standing in front of her on the street, quivering.

I slept on it. I went back to bed again. You have to understand, I slept on it, I thought about it. And I woke up, and I think I don't agree. And I won't stop. I'll not only kick in your garden gate, I'll also kick in the door to your house. I'll trample your entire life to pieces; it's something I can do. You'll lie under the bedcovers and bite your fingernails; your teeth will chatter.

Stella hears him, but can't comprehend any of it. She holds onto the gate and hears something in Mister Pfister's speech tip over and then splinter. His mother. Every evening. The nights. Hooks and systems, the police, as far as she can follow him, he is inviting her to go to the police. She listens – it's like listening to Walter – and she sees in his face the splintering of the words; she can actually read it, and she can also see that he senses this and wants to hold it back and cannot hold it back. He looks awful. And in spite of that Stella thinks that she wants to kill Mister Pfister, shoot him, beat him to death, stomp on him, cut him into pieces like paper, here and now, on the spot. To stop this. So that it can just stop.

Mister Pfister breaks off. Livid.

He says, Register a complaint. Register a complaint now, go ahead.

I will, Stella says. I'll do it.

Twenty-one

I've painted Chinese motifs on two silk foulards, Clara writes to Stella, *lotus blossoms and birds, but there's something else hidden among the lotus and the birds, something very tiny, rather ugly; you have to search for it. One scarf for you and one for me. Alma is having a lot of trouble getting used to kindergarten, and Ricky is losing all his teeth at the same time; it's really a strange arrangement, don't you think, all those nights awake with screaming babies when they're getting their milk teeth, and five years later they simply spit them all out again. Do you remember Ava's toothless baby smile? How tired we were then? Alma's teacher tells me that Alma is still very childish, and I could have said, Yes, what the hell else is she supposed to be; after all, she's still a child. I always think of such answers too late, only after we're already home again. Luckily I'm very busy;*

otherwise I'd just take Alma out of there. But I have to finish two pictures, and I completed the sketch for the mermaid; the mermaid has your face. After I've cast her, you'll have to come and baptise her. Ava is allowed to pick a name for her. If the children don't see each other soon, they'll walk right past each other on the street later on and not even recognise each other. That's a horrible thought, I find. But maybe they'll recognise each other after all? Recognise something in the other, something indefinite, like a vague memory of something that once was. We ordered wood for the winter; the man who delivered the wood just let it slide out of the truck onto the middle of the lawn, and now I'm stacking the wood into piles; there's no better work in the world. Stupid and good. The smell of the wood is wonderful, arranging the pieces of wood, extremely calming. Actually, from now on I want to do only things like this. Cleaning up, tidying, sorting, carting off. Is that idiotic? What would you say? I think the older I get, the more I simply want to have my peace and quiet. I want to sit in peace at my kitchen table and smoke, think-ing about this and that; I'd never have thought that this would one day be so important to me. The children keep pulling me away from it. That's the way it is. Quartering apples. Doing laundry, ironing shirts. Before, I used to be able to imagine being someone else. Today I'm only myself. Tired and overextended. But in spite of that the foulards turned out gorgeous, and I keep thinking of you; it feels as if you had just gone out for a little while and would come back right away. I keep thinking you'll come right back. Stella, how are you? Are the ravens still flying around the tower?

*

I'd like you to pack your things, Jason says on the phone.

I'd like you to pack a bag with sweaters and socks and books for you and for Ava, and I'd like you to get out of there. Go to the country, go to Paloma's house; stay there a while. I'd like it if, for once, you'd listen to me and do what I say. Just one single time.

When haven't I listened to you, Stella thinks. What's that supposed to mean. Were there ever any moments when I should have listened to you, done what you said and instead did something else? What?

She listens to Jason, does what he says. Packs a bag, sweaters and socks, Ava's hedgehog, two toothbrushes and seven books. Sets the bag down in the front hall. Puts Ava's rain jacket on top of the bag, puts her rubber boots next to it.

*

This place, the bicycle mechanic says, was here before you, and it'll still be here after you're gone. Places do something to you, but you don't do anything to them. This development will remain whether you happen to be here or not. Your house will continue to be a house; it won't turn to ashes after you walk out the door for the last time. Everything you feel or experience takes place only within you; there's only the 'inside us' – nothing else. This is sobering. But also obvious – you are the constant.

He sets the wheel he's just put the spokes into rolling. The wheel rolls evenly. Sunlight catches in the spokes and is flung out.

*

Well, there are this kind of stars and that kind, Ava says. Really little ones with lots of points and regular stars with five points; she indicates the points with the fingers of her left hand. Aunt

Sonja says all the stars have been dead for a long time; what's that supposed to mean anyway. I broke my hairslide, my hairslide is gone now. I'd like to have curly hair some day, very long, curly hair, just once. When you were a child, you didn't want to be called Stella. Papa told me. You wanted to be called Silvia. Is that right? Is that really true? I only like your food and Papa's food. I never want to eat in the kindergarten again. Oh, how Stevie can laugh. You have to hear that sometime. Can we drive to the sea? Can we drive to see Papa at the construction site? Will this summer get even hotter? I wished it would always be very hot. We went to the puppet theatre today, and do you know what they had – the play with the three little pigs and the wolf. I want to stay here. Here there's Stevie. I never want to leave here. Never!

*

The police officer who takes the complaint has melancholy eyes and a moustache, his shirt is wrinkled and he looks as if he'd been on duty for twenty-four hours. He has to leave the room when Stella bursts into tears – she breaks into tears like Ava, can scarcely speak through her sobbing – but he comes back bringing a little packet of tissues and a cup of hot, sweet tea with milk. His office is dreary, the windows are high up below the ceiling, impossible to get a view outside. In spite of that, there's a plant on his desk, and there are postcards on the wall from the Canary Islands, Mexican pyramids, just as in Paloma's office.

Stella is interrogated. She is supposed to provide detailed information, but she considers it an interrogation.

Since when do you know Mister Pfister.

I don't know Mister Pfister at all.

Didn't you meet him?

I meet him every day. He rings at our house every day, but I still don't know him; he is fixated on me without knowing me. Don't you understand what I'm saying; can't you imagine what this is like, can't you?

Yes, yes, I know what you mean, I can imagine it, the police officer says, trying to sound reassuring and looking at Stella sceptically. He says, But in spite of that, we have to write it all down step by step, from the beginning.

And Stella pushes the shoebox across the desk; she hands it over. She describes the bell-ringing, the things in the mailbox, the encounter at the shopping centre, the first and the last conversation between her and Mister Pfister. She watches the policeman as he takes the scraps and pieces of paper, the matches, lighters, CDs and dictation machine, and the photos out of the shoebox, and even as he is reformulating and summarising her sentences and entering them into his computer, she can see the shock, anger and fear disintegrate.

Not communicable. The bicycle mechanic had already understood this; that there is only what's inside us, nothing else.

In spite of that, she says, Do you believe me? I mean do you believe me when I say that I can't stand it?

The policeman says, I believe you. I can also tell you that you have every reason for coming here. It's just that you're coming rather late, I think. By the way, what is your profession?

Nurse, Stella says. I'm a nurse.

She thinks that she can read in the policeman's face that her profession explains some things for him. Nurses are very stable, but they have a helper syndrome. Can't defend themselves very well, are always somewhat slow on the uptake.

I have a child, Stella says. I'm married. She says it as if it would change something.

The policeman goes to the toilet, and Stella waits until she can no longer hear his footsteps in the corridor; then she leans forward and turns the computer screen so she can look at it.

The woman making the complaint is visibly affected by the incidents.

Visibly affected.

This sentence is a gift. Stella sees it, accepts it, and turns the screen back to its original position, puts her hands in her lap and waits.

*

What came of it, Jason says on the phone.

We'll have to wait and see, Stella says. They're going to go to his place and tell him that from this moment on it will be a punishable offence if he approaches me in any way. They call it a de-escalation visit. They told me that according to previous experience the situation will get worse following the de-escalation visit.

Good grief, Jason says. What kind of people are they sending over there.

Policemen specialised in dealing with hooligans, Stella says. In a certain way it feels wonderful to be able to say it like that.

Well then, I'll set off, Jason says after a while. I'll get going. I'll drive home first and then I'll drive out to the country to see you. Take care of yourself, Stella.

Till soon, Stella says off-handedly. OK then, see you soon. Take care!

*

I'm glad that you wanted to say goodbye to me, Esther says
pleasantly. That's gone completely out of style, saying farewell
like that; people think it's not at all necessary to say goodbye any
more. Good-bye. She draws the word out scornfully. We two
have to think of another farewell word, for we'll never see each
other again. Not in this life at least. What shall we say – Adieu?
Well, it's not time yet anyway. I've made myself beautiful for
you, did you notice?

Esther is wearing a sweater with silver and gold threads over
her pyjamas; she picked this sweater out herself and put it on,
then fiercely insisted on making it to the living room by herself.
She's painted her cheeks red and combed her hair in all direc-
tions, draped a necklace of ivory elephants around her neck; she
looks like a feverish clown.

Yes, Stella says. I noticed. You look smashing; thank you.

Esther laughs, as if she knew better. Open the left cupboard
door, please. Take out two glasses, not those tiny round ones,
the big cut-glass ones are the right ones. You can choose what
you prefer, blackcurrant or cherry; I always liked blackcurrant best. You'll have to reach down, the bottles are at the very
bottom, at the back. Move them around a little, farther to the
left. There, wonderful, I had no idea that there was so much left
in the bottle.

Actually it isn't permitted, Stella says.

Exactly, Esther says. Actually it isn't permitted.

Stella fills both glasses.

Right up to the very top, Esther says; never hesitate! All of
life is an abyss, and the less afraid you are and the longer you

look down into it, the more you'll enjoy it. You'll come to realise that one day; I consider you somewhat less dim-witted than all the others. Cheers.

The alcohol is sweet and strong; Stella feels it immediately in her legs and in her head, a spaced-out heaviness in the middle of the day at noon. Esther smacks her lips. She takes the bottle from Stella and pours the glasses full a second time. She says, You could eat an apple with it. You look like someone who always eats apples. I never ate apples. Never.

She leans to one side and with an amazingly forceful gesture brushes the pile of old newspapers off the sofa and onto the floor. I have something for you, a little farewell gift; where is it; I hid it here, I'm quite sure. She pushes the boxes of sweets aside, lifts up the cushions. Here it is. Please take it with you; put it in your handbag, which, by the way, is much too big.

It's a little box. A rectangular little box of brown wood, cherrywood perhaps, as small as a coffin for a mouse.

Stella opens the cover and looks inside. The box is empty.

Of course it's empty, Esther says triumphantly. Save something in it. The first thing that matters to you in your new life – put it in there, and check on it from time to time; perhaps it will change into something else. I wish you all the best, I really do; you may trust me on that. And you've got problems trusting people, or am I mistaken?

Twenty-two

On Sunday morning the bells of the village church peal outside the window of the room in which Stella and Ava are sleeping. Ava is sleeping so deeply it's as if she were recovering from something. For a long time Stella lies on her side looking at her. Ava's dreamy face has an expression from which she has difficulty disengaging. Then she gets up. There's a fire glowing in the stove in the kitchen; on the table stands a silver pot of coffee; Paloma is in church. Stella goes out into the garden; it finally rained during the night, and the grass is still wet and cold. She stands behind the crooked garden fence looking down the country road. The road comes from the village, runs past the house, up the hill, and into the unknown on the other side of the hill. The windmills on the horizon begin haltingly to turn. The pine trees in the garden creak the same way as those back home. Smoke from the kitchen fire rises from the chimney, hovers above the roof, and then dissipates under the sky.

*

The previous evening Mister Pfister swept all his papers into a large pile behind his house, all the paper, the newspapers, pads, notebooks, reams of wrapping paper, direct mail, cardboard, absolutely all the photos, as well as the heavy red envelopes, even those. Someone called the police. The police came by and politely but firmly kept Mister Pfister from lighting the pile. During the night the words, the headlines, pictures, chains of thoughts and questions, the insoluble puzzles, all this got thoroughly soaked by the rain and finally and conclusively dissolved.

Mister Pfister was taken to police headquarters around ten o'clock that night. He was able to credibly assure the police at headquarters that he was simply at the end of his tether, nothing more. He was simply at the end of his tether; something like that can happen; it was all just too much for him; he needed to get some rest; it will pass. Everything's all right. No need to worry. He can promise them that; he'll come to grips with it.

He was also informed that Stella had registered a complaint.

Who?

Stella. A nurse by profession, thirty-seven years of age, married, the mother of a child.

Oh, yes.

He will receive a summons next week and was informed that from now on he would be committing an offence with each attempt to make contact with Stella. With each attempt. With every message, every request for forgiveness. With no matter what. Mister Pfister took note of it. Also signed a statement saying that he had taken note of it, had written his name in his feminine handwriting. He was sent home from police head-quarters in the early morning hours. His path led past Stella's house; there was no way around that; of course he rang the bell at her door, all the windows remained dark, the situation is the same as it was.

Now he is home and demolishing his house from the inside, from the inside to the outside at a deliberate pace. He destroys the furniture, taking it apart, hacking it up, throwing it all out, chair and table through the window over the sink and out into the garden, followed by cups, bottles and glasses, rubbish, blankets, shoes. Until nothing is left. Mister Pfister then wraps himself up in the last remaining blanket and lies down on the floor. The wind blows into the house through the smashed windows.

*

Ava sleeps till almost midday; then she calls Stella. Stella sits down on the edge of the bed. Ava says, Good morning. Stella feels that Ava is suddenly old enough to know that it can be nice to say good morning. Maybe she doesn't know it yet, but she has an inkling already. Good Morning. She helps Ava get dressed and goes into the kitchen with her; Ava wants to take her hedgehog along; reaching for Stella's hand she behaves as formally as at the beginning of a children's birthday party.

Paloma is back from church and has set the table with her best dishes; the teacups are dark blue with stars glittering at the bottom. There is marble cake with raspberries she picked herself, apricots and chocolate cream to go with it. Ava sitting on three pillows says, I'm as hungry as a wolf. Do you know how hungry a wolf gets?

Paloma who seems softer and more tired here in her own house than in her life in town, pours Ava some hot cocoa and pushes the sugar bowl close to her cup. She says, If you want to, we could go to the lake. We could go swimming and see what the beaver is doing. Paloma is usually alone in this house, going to the lake alone, watching the beaver alone, drinking her tea alone, but surely not from the dark-blue cups. Or maybe she does?

I heard a raven, Ava says; she tilts her head, opens her eyes wide, and raises her index finger; did you hear it too.

That's my house raven, Paloma says. If you're lucky, he'll do a trick for you; he's a performer; he can turn around himself twice in flight.

Stella feels so numb that she's almost happy. As if this kitchen were an island; who would have expected that. She is grateful to Paloma for the fact that she apparently doesn't intend to say anything about the present situation, nothing about the real reason for Stella and Ava's visit. But on the other hand, Stella wishes Paloma *would* say something about it, ask about it, that there were some possibility of it, like a way out.

We have a stalker, Ava says. She turns away from Stella as if she'd read her mind, as if it was finally time. She spits out an apricot pip and puts her hands over the ears of the hedgehog in her lap.

We have a stalker; what does he actually look like?

Unremarkable, Stella says. He looks unremarkable, quite normal, like you and me. If we see him on the street, I'll point him out to you. But actually you don't have to know what he looks like; we won't be meeting him any more. And you mustn't be afraid.

She meets Paloma's gaze, the alert, intent look in her eyes.

*

Early Sunday afternoon, Mister Pfister, who had slept in his clothes, puts his shoes back on. He kicks some object out of the way, reaches for the last bottle of beer, and goes out, leaving the door and the gate wide open behind him.

He walks past the bicycle mechanic's house without looking at it. The bicycle mechanic is not there either, having driven, as he does every Sunday, to the countryside. Mister Pfister walks along the street; the hunchbacked, keen-eyed child crosses his path as always, crossing from right to left, not looking at him and disappearing into the now luxuriant garden. Mister Pfister can hear people talking to one another. The clatter of coffee cups from the shady terraces, a murmur. He can hear dogs barking far off; he hears the wind in the field.

An overcast afternoon sun above Stella's house. No car in the driveway, the front door closed, the dormer window open, but the orange flag has been run up.

No one in sight.

No one is in sight. Is Stella home?

In the course of yesterday evening, the hours at the police station, the amazing conversations, the clean-up, the rearranging, the morning on the floor wrapped in the old blanket, Mister Pfister had lost touch a little. The general picture. He's slightly off-kilter, but that can be remedied; it can be re-established. He stops in front of the gate and looks it over. He looks at it very closely. And this time he doesn't ring, he simply omits the ringing and instead just kicks the garden gate open; he just kicks it open for the second time, the same way as on the day with the photo of the bed, a picture from another time, and he... and here he just can't think any further; here his thoughts break off. The gate swings open; Mister Pfister steps into the garden. Opalescent, drastic colours and over the colours, the fantastic humming of insects. Stella's house begins to sway. Something pushes the glass panes outward from inside. Pebbles and old screws jump up off the stairs in front of the door to the house; that child's penchant for junk; the spade leaning against the brick wall slips sidewards; the red brick wall glows from the heat. Mister Pfister has now reached the front door. He could ring here; after all he's never rung the bell here. He could give her one very last chance to open the door like a damned totally normal human being and say, Hello. Nice that you passed by, come in, sit down, what can I offer you. Does she deserve a very last chance.

Stella. Thirty-seven years old, a nurse by profession, married, mother of a child.

She doesn't.

Mister Pfister takes a running jump, taking the stairs in one leap and throwing himself against the door so hard that the walls tremble. He keeps kicking at the door at the level of the lock, against the dry, white-painted wood, against the leaded glass panes, which surprisingly don't yield. Then he takes a break. Stands still, out of breath, waiting. The door opens.

*

Jason stands in the doorway. He is holding the stick Stevie gave Ava, the stick with which Ava practises kata for Stevie, bunkai, shotokan, H-shaped base lines, star-shaped base lines; the stick is heavy and solid. Ava practised in front of the house last week, strolled back into the house, dropped the stick on the floor, and went to the kitchen to have a glass of ice-cold lemonade. Stella picked up the stick and propped it against the wall next to the coat rack. Jason took the stick, and with this stick in his hand finally opened the door.

He strikes out immediately. Raises the stick, hauls back, and strikes out. He strikes Mister Pfister from the top of the front steps back out to the driveway; at first it's easy to beat him back to the driveway because Mister Pfister is quite surprised, but then he suddenly starts yelling and fends off Jason's blows, yelling.

Jason hits his knees, his back, his spine, his shoulders. But only after Mister Pfister manages to break the bottle, which he simply hasn't wanted to let go of, on the top step, and then tries to ram the broken-off neck of the bottle into Jason's belly, does Jason bash him on the head.

He whacks the stick against his skull and Mister Pfister goes down, lets go of the bottle neck, kicks at Jason, already holding up his hands, but then keeps kicking at Jason, slobbering and screaming. Pretty soon the bright pebbles in front of the stair landing are full of blood. Mister Pfister skidded through the broken glass and apparently also has a hole in his head. He wets his pants. The smell of linden, clover, of urine, sweat and shit. It seems that Jason for one moment – it's a golden moment – just can't stop himself any more from bashing Mister Pfister's skull. Solemnly smashing this skull, he keeps hitting it. Again. Over and over again.

Then it passes.

Jason grabs Mister Pfister by his dirty, warm, bloody, wet sweater and drags him down the driveway, away from the front door towards the gate; he drags him out onto the pavement and leaves him lying there. He goes back into the house, throws the bottle neck, the glass shards into the rubbish bin, puts the stick back in the hall, and locks the front door, which shows the clear traces of Mister Pfister's shoe soles, behind him. He walks out of the garden into the street. Mister Pfister is sitting up, leaning against the fence; he is crying, his face is smeared with blood; with his right arm he holds his left arm away from his body; his hands are bloody and he's spitting blood as Jason passes him.

Then he collapses. Something trails over the asphalt, Mister Pfister's sobbing sounds childish, then stops.

*

Jason walks down Forest Lane.

The street has a Sunday feel. Everything remains behind.

*

Stella, Paloma and Ava are on their way to the lake when Stella's mobile phone rings. The path is swampy and muddy; the beaver has dammed the lake and cut down the willows; sedge grows high between the tree stumps. The path is enchanted; ducks start up out of the reeds; Ava, picking cowslips and arum, walks far ahead.

It's already getting dark a little earlier, Paloma says. I'm afraid of the early dark; the summer is much too short.

Yes, Stella says, this summer has been short.

The phone rings dully in the basket with the bathing suits,

towels, suntan lotion, and Stella takes it out carefully, reading the name of the policeman with the melancholy eyes on the display. She turns away from Paloma; Paloma keeps walking.

Hello, Stella says.

The policeman says, I'm standing in your house. It's a nice house. Where are you; are you all right? Are you all right?

I'm all right, Stella says. She looks around her at the reeds, the dark lakeside landscape, the intense green tones. Ava and Paloma at the end of the path, waving. Stella waves back. She says, Why are you standing in my house.

She can picture the policeman in her kitchen. The table, Ava's crayons, the little board with apple peels, cores, the lake pebble from Jason; are the beds made upstairs; is the bathroom neat; what could betray her; she pictures the policeman standing in her kitchen like a statue: a freeze frame. As if her entire life had been headed towards this one image.

He says, There was an argument here. An escalation. Someone called the police, and there was so much blood in your front yard that we thought something had happened to you. Do you understand me. Can you hear me?

Was the house broken into, Stella says. I understand you very well; I can hear you. Why are you standing in my house?

Your house was locked, and we broke in because we thought you were inside. We thought you were … injured, the policeman says; he says it very guardedly.

I am uninjured, Stella says. I'm not injured. I'm in the country, far away; I'm fine.

Well then, the policeman says. Mister Pfister is in the hospital. He's not doing well at all. Did he smash his skull himself? Do you know anything about it? We're having a new lock put in here. We'll get back to you. Please stay where you are, if you can afford it. Will you do that?

Yes, Stella says, I'll try. Several different images collide and separate again in her mind, making no sense. Where is Jason. Mister Pfister's smashed skull looking like a bony bowl full of sooty leaves. Stella says, Is the house empty. I mean – was there no one in the house, was the house empty.

Yes, the policeman says, the house was empty. Well, let's say – it was as empty as a lived-in house can be.

I can't talk on the phone any more, Stella says. I'm going to hang up now.

The path ahead of her is deserted. Paloma and Ava must have turned off into the field. Stella stands there a while longer. It's as if something had ended, as if something were beginning anew.

Twenty-three

Later, Stella sometimes thinks about how powerful Jason's blows must have been. What these blows were really all about. She's thinking about this as she's packing dishes, plates and cups, the cover of the sugar bowl and the sugar bowl, the teapot, the cereal bowls, the glasses with the floral pattern, wrapping them in newspaper, putting them in cardboard boxes, sealing the cardboard boxes and with a grease pencil writing the word *Fragile* on the top, over and over again – Fragile.

She comes to no conclusion.

She empties her desk, all the while still thinking about it; she puts the books she no longer wants to read into boxes, and other books that she still loves into different boxes, and she sorts her letters into files – Clara's letters, the few precious letters from

Jason, letters from people who are already dead – and, after lengthy hesitation, writes on the backs of the files: beautiful letters.

She thinks about it all until the man from the municipal utilities comes to the door and rings the bell; he's come to read the electric and gas meters, and she stands next to him watching as he enters the numbers representing her use of heat and light on a form, as if it were the most ordinary thing in the world.

She packs up Ava's things. She sets aside the things Ava has grown out of, puts the things she can still wear right now into the suitcase, and while Ava isn't there she carts off the toys Ava doesn't play with any more. She keeps all the stuffed animals. Carefully she detaches the mobile from the ceiling, folds up the princess dress and packs it even though it's too small now. She saves all of Ava's books. Her favourite book – *that's the blue door let's see who lives there, we'll just knock / someone home / seven monkeys / what do seven monkeys do / monkey business* – she stands at the window in Ava's room with the open book, wondering whether, while he was hitting out at Mr Pfister with the stick, Jason was thinking of her, whether Jason as he was landing all those blows was thinking of Stella.

She finds a drawing by Jason among Ava's books. He had drawn Stella – as seen from Ava's room – sitting on the chair in the garden at the edge of the meadow, Stella in profile in her grey dress and barefoot, her hair down and hands in her lap; at the bottom he had written the date and her name as if he wanted to be sure who she was. As if he never wanted to forget her.

*

As she steps out of the house, she can see Jason, a lover, bent over Mister Pfister. She doesn't want to see it like that, but she does see it. She thinks about removing the three names from the mailbox with turpentine; she leaves them there.

*

She writes her last letter to Clara from this house sitting on top of a box in the emptied-out kitchen with the letter paper on her knees; she writes, *Dear Clara, if I hadn't caught your bouquet, everything might have turned out completely different; jasmine and lilac, do you actually still remember? I think it's unfair that the connection between things can only be recognised and understood in retrospect. And on the other hand, I'm glad, I have a wild and confident heart. I'm about to hand in the keys; once I walk through this door I'll never look back again, not once, I swear. And I think – where I'll be tomorrow, today is already over. Take care of yourself! Think of me, your –*

*

Left behind are the pencil lines marking Ava's growth. Date and centimetres, a memory that exists only for Stella of an evening in March, of a winter day, of an afternoon with rain. The shadow on the wall where the bookshelf stood, the marks left by the picture frames in Jason's room, that light spot on the banister where Stella supported herself morning after morning, going down to the kitchen to put the kettle on, to begin an ordinary day. Remaining are Ava's little decals on the windowpane. The blue wall. The dried lavender tied with package twine on the windowsill, the little paper horse next to it. A shekel, a shell, a coin on the rim of the sandpit. Mullein, lupines.

*

Much later, as if from a great distance, Stella remembers the years in the development, that time in her life. The house, the rooms, the view of the open field from the kitchen window, the morning light and sky are locked inside a capsule, forever out of reach. She can see it all from the outside, but she can't touch it, and she is surprised at how little she lacks. She lacks – nothing. Or only what she would be lacking anyway. Maybe it really is the present that counts, its light, irresistible weight; Stella is at home wherever she lives and wherever she sleeps. It is possible to leave places, to drop promises. She can still come out of the bedroom with her eyes closed, go down the stairs into the kitchen, and put the kettle on before she turns on the radio, and yet she feels no longing. This means she could leave again any time. Change is not a betrayal. And even if it were, it wouldn't be punished.

*

Stella, Jason says, are you awake? Look out the window, if you can.

What would I see if I could, Stella says.

*

An incredibly huge, orange-yellow half-moon, a hand's breadth above the horizon.